UNBREAK HER HEART

SMALL TOWN SECOND-CHANCE ROMANCE

BRIE WILDS

RUTTISH
PRESS

No part of this book may be reproduced in any form or by any electronic or mechanical means, including information storage and retrieval systems, without written permission from the author, except for the use of brief quotations in a book review.

Published by Ruttish Press, Sparta

eISBN: 978-1-63589-749-4
ISBN: 978-1-63589-750-0

Editor: Kasi Alexander
Cover Design: Brie Wilds

GET MY NEWSLETTER
Want to receive the latest information on my upcoming novels and receive a FREE book? Sign up for my newsletter by clicking on Brie Wilds Newsletter or visit www.briewilds.com

1

Luke

IT WAS A SLOW SUMMER NIGHT, THE TYPE LUKE LIKED. His leg rested lazily on the gas pedal, feeding the engine just enough gas to maintain that unhurried rush.

The Grand Cherokee moved lazily on Route 15, eating up the remaining asphalt to Beaver Run like a turtle on steroids. That the old car made it this far impressed Luke, and he was thankful. Money was tight.

He likened his return to Beaver Run to that of the prodigal son. But there wouldn't be anyone waiting to slaughter a cow or call a feast in his honor. All he had left were ghosts. Two in the cemetery, the third whereabouts unknown. Yet he couldn't keep away. When the option came to decide where to work next, he'd picked the small town where he grew up.

The hum of the air conditioner and a soft summer tune coming from the radio reminded Luke of the summer nights he'd spent in Beaver Run as a kid. Back then, the summer seemed endless.

He checked his rearview mirror. There was no car behind him. The farther north he went, the more the traffic thinned out.

He studied his reflection-bags under his eyes, with two days' worth of stubble on his chin and cheeks. He ran his hand through his thick black hair and brushed it to the left, then to the right. He could pass for scruffy sexy.

Luke sighed and looked outside the window to the dark horizon. The sky was so clear the moon looked like a flashlight suspended in an almost dark room. His eyes drifted between the road and the sky, always making sure there were no cars close enough ahead before taking his eyes away from the road.

The trees and bushes he passed looked like a welcome parade. They lined up, waiting in anticipation, appearing and disappearing. Was it really worth it going to Beaver Run to paint? He should have done more research, found another location with a drawbridge, close to a lake and forest, and gone there. But somewhere familiar always trumped a strange place.

A loud chirping cricket sound cut through the silence in the car. Luke looked at his phone mounted on the dash stand with a magnet. His stomach lurched. It was one of the guys from the bed and breakfast he'd stayed at while visiting Grand Marais, Minnesota.

If he answered, he'd have to apologize and tell him where he was. If he didn't answer, the guy would call again. In fact, Luke was surprised he was only just calling now after two days. He exhaled, tapped the phone, and put it through the car's speakers via Bluetooth. "Hello."

"Luke? Jesus! What happened?" he sounded squeaky.

"Hello, Leonardo."

"Hello? Is that all you have to say? We've been worried sick the past two days. You just vanished. Where are you?"

"Sorry, something came up, and I had to go. Where am I?" He looked around, debating whether to tell him where he was. He didn't lie to people, just left without notice. He decided to tell. "Somewhere in New Jersey."

"New Jersey? Wow." There was a pause. "Just as we were just getting to know you. That means you're not exhibiting your work?"

"Really sorry…it was an emergency."

"When are you coming back?"

Luke knew he wasn't coming back. This time he curved the truth. "Not sure, but I'll keep in touch. Sorry, I have to go. My regards to everybody. Bye." He hung up.

Goodbyes were tough. His way was the best. Just pack up and go.

A car coming in the opposite direction with its lights at full beam dipped them as if averting its eyes and saying, *Here comes the unworthy.*

Luke shook his head and smiled. Was he too hard on himself? Always on the move. Spend time at a place. Once people started to know him, he would uproot himself. In the past six years, that seemed to be his way of life.

"At the next turn, make a right," said the female voice of the car's navigation system.

Luke was pulled out of his reverie. He looked at the phone screen-15 minutes from his final destination. He let out a sigh of relief just as his pulse rate shot up a notch. He was almost there.

He might just be lucky, sneak into town, make sketches in the woods, then do the painting indoors. Staying in the house wouldn't be difficult-he had just enough money to pay the model and buy a ton of ramen noodles.

Once he was done with the painting, Bill Madden would show up, collect the art, and release the money in escrow, then he would leave without interacting with local folks.

Luke felt like it had been so long he'd been away that it was unlikely people would recognize him, and he them.

He felt a vibration on the wheel and gripped the steering wheel tighter. Was that real, or his mind playing tricks on him? He glanced at the dash-the fuel gauge showed he had enough gas. The temperature was fine. The car was not overheating, and the tire pressures were fine.

The Cherokee's headlamps fell on a sign that said *Welcome to Beaver Run. Est. 1796*.

He'd finally arrived. Now, if everything went according to plan, it might just be in and out without anyone noticing he was there.

His head darted from side to side like a kid in a candy shop. Even though it was nighttime, Luke recognized some buildings. It was still the same houses on that particular street. Maybe the occupants had changed. The bushes and trees were familiar.

Luke fought the urge to drive to the street where he grew up and look at his old house. Who lived there now? He had two weeks in Beaver Run. Maybe sometime before he left.

Luke's stomach rumbled, reminding him that the last time he'd eaten was three hours ago. The calories from that burger were now a distant memory. He should have loaded up on granola bars when he stopped to pee in Pennsylvania.

There was a restaurant on Main Street that was on his way. He might get some food if it was still there. At this time of the night, he would just be another customer passing through. Nobody would recognize him. Even the guy he rented the Airbnb from didn't recognize his name.

Luke decided against it. The house owner had said the

fridge would be fully stocked. Luke reckoned there must be something there he could eat.

He was giddy with excitement. When he stopped at a light, he tapped his phone to check his email to see if the model he'd booked for the nude painting had responded on when she would get to New Jersey.

There was nothing from her.

A pair of lights in the rearview mirror caught his eyes as a car approached from behind. He'd send a reminder. He typed quickly.

In NJ. R we still on schedule?

He hit send just as the light turned green.

Luke pressed down on the gas pedal, and the Cherokee moved forward. For the next few minutes, he gazed out of the window, taking in the scenes.

"In five hundred feet, make a right."

Luke glanced at the GPS. He knew the street the Airbnb was on but not the exact house. Right now, he could turn off the navigation. But she'd been a great companion. Luke pushed the signal to indicate he'd be making a right.

"Turn right onto Main Street."

Luke slowed and made the turn. He accelerated and picked up speed. A few moments later, his car jerked and slowed. Luke stepped on the gas. It moved, then seconds later, jerked again.

The car behind him honked its horn, then pulled out from behind Luke's car and overtook him.

"Asshole!" yelled a passenger from the car as it sped past him.

Luke stepped down on the pedal, but the car wasn't responding. "What the...? His eyes darted to the dashboard. Everything looked normal. He looked for the hazard button, found it, and pushed it. "Come on, come on. Not now. We're almost there." His breathing was quick and shallow. His stomach tied in knots.

The car lunged forward, then slowed again. This it did a few times.

Luke drifted to the side of the road. Cars passed him. Then he saw a parking lot to his right, and the entrance was just ahead. He turned the car in and guided it into a spot. The engine sputtered and died.

Luke took a deep breath and exhaled noisily through his mouth. "Shit." He sighed again and said in a game show presenter's voice, "Welcome to Beaver Run." He turned the key off, then back on. Nothing happened. No sound. No lights came on.

Luke took in his surroundings. It was the parking lot of a restaurant and bar called Beaver Tail. He might as well get something to eat. Maybe the car would start after the engine had cooled.

The thump thump thump of the music, the sound of cutlery and people having conversations hit Luke once he opened the door. He could have been in an Olive Garden anywhere in the US.

The receptionist smiled. "Hello."

Luke smiled back. "Hi there. Dinner for one."

She nodded and grabbed a leather-bound menu. "Please follow me." She took him to a table for two. "Enjoy."

Luke sat down. Soon a waitress came and took his order. "Double cheeseburger, fries, and a Coke."

"Coming right up," said the waitress and left.

Luke looked around and saw the sign for the bathroom. He headed there, peed, and washed his face with cold water. After patting it dry with a paper towel and finger-combing his hair, he felt better. He went back to his chair; nobody paid him any attention.

Moments later, his food arrived. This time it was a different waitress.

"Hi, I'm Laura. I'll be your waitress for the evening."

"Hi Laura," said Luke. Their eyes met. There was something familiar about her. "I'm Luke." He saw it in her eyes too.

"Pleased to meet you. If there's anything you need, don't hesitate to ask." She smiled and walked away.

Luke heaved a sigh of relief. Just a friendly person. He took a sip of Coke and attacked the food. It quickly disappeared, and he felt better. The food was great.

As he sipped his drink, Laura came back and said, "I've been thinking. You look like someone I went to high school with."

2

Luke

THE WAITRESS WAGGED A FINGER AT HIM. "LUKE! LUKE Martin."

"Yes," said Luke. His head jerked up, and he felt his stomach tighten.

"You don't remember me?"

Luke put on a *Yes, you've caught me* smile. "I know I should, but forgive me, it's been such a long time I was back here. I'm a total ass. Please remind me."

"High school…I'm Laura-"

Luke gasped. "Laura Paterson. It's a pleasure to see you again."

"Same here! Wow, welcome back."

"Thank you."

"I'm sorry…I heard about your father," said Laura.

"Oh yes. Thank you. Yeah, he was really sick. He fought the good fight."

"Are you back for good, or…?"

Luke chuckled inside at the way the question hinted for what he was doing now. "No, I'm here for work, actually. I'm painting some landscapes around Beaver Run."

Laura nodded. "Thinking of it, we have gorgeous forests around here."

They had that awkward moment when nothing is said by both parties.

Luke remembered his car predicament. "Listen, my car died as I got here. Do you guys have a cab service I could call?"

"Cars and their problems. I've had my own share of car trouble. Where are you going?"

He told her.

Laura grinned. "That's Stone's Airbnb. He's one of the deputy sheriffs. Moved here not too long ago. Now he more or less lives on the Williams farm."

"That's *WAY* out," said Luke.

Laura shrugged. "Well, he's engaged to Adela. He's accepted the reality that he's in love and moved in with her. That's what men in love do, not run away from people they love."

Did she know about him? It depends on the circumstance, but he didn't say that out loud. Her next words almost knocked him over.

Laura raised a finger. "Hey, wait a minute." Her eyes lit up. "Weren't you dating Sandra? Sandra Leigh in high school? And you guys continued on in college."

"Emmm…yeah. It…it didn't work out after college."

"Life happens. Anyway, let me look into helping you get to Stone's place. I'll be right back."

Luke watched her leave. She turned back once to look at him with a twinkle in her eyes, like she was making sure he wasn't going anywhere. She wasn't bad, but the last thing he wanted to do in Beaver Run was come back and get himself embroiled with a woman.

It then dawned on him that his cover was blown. It hadn't taken long. By tomorrow the whole town would know that Dave Martin's prodigal son was back.

He exhaled and sat back in his chair. Well, he might as well relax and embrace the experience. He looked around, nodding his head to the music. It wasn't a bad joint. This was probably his first time coming in here. It was nice. He was thinking of elaborate ways to avoid people when Laura returned.

Laura smiled. "You're in luck. My colleague's going the same way as you. Can you be ready in ten minutes?"

Luke felt like a big weight had been lifted off his shoulder. "Oh, thank you so much. I'm ready right now."

Laura giggled. "Ten minutes, okay?"

Luke nodded. "Thank you so much. You're a lifesaver."

"I'll take that as a compliment. It was nice seeing you after all these years. Anyway, I have to go. How long are you around for?"

Luke crossed his fingers. "Two weeks."

"Please drop by again." She waved and walked away.

Luke tapped his phone and opened a browser. He would need a mechanic as soon as possible. Someone had to take a look at his car and get it moving again. His best-laid plans had just been trashed even before he started. He would need a car to get around.

Why did the car decide to pack up now? Right at the end of the long trip. Luke sighed again and typed in *mechanic Beaver Run NJ* and hit search.

Not finding anything promising on Google, Luke took a deep breath and looked up. Time stood still.

Staring at him was none other than Sandra Leigh. It was

as if the universe had ears and had been listening. Mention someone's name, and they appeared from nowhere.

She'd probably seen him first and was about to flee. Or maybe it wasn't her. No, he knew that face like the back of his hands. He'd traced his finger up and down the contours of that face. Traced her lips with his fingers and moaned in ecstasy when those lips did things to him. He could draw her whole body with his eyes shut.

Luke took her in, from her head, down and back up again. She now wore her natural blond hair longer. All that baby fat was gone. She looked chiseled and toned. Matured like fine wine. He knew every contour of that body and would love to take her in his arms again. But he'd really fucked up the last time.

3

Sandra

Earlier that evening Sandra worked the bar. She pulled the trigger, and white foam shot out of the tap into the mug. Another image came to her mind-it had been a long time since she'd gotten laid. The foam changed to liquid amber as the glass filled, dragging her mind out of the gutter.

She filled two more mugs with tap beer as she scanned the room. The crowd was a mixture of town folks and people she hadn't seen before. Vacationers were now learning that this county was not only a winter paradise. Summers were great too, and the crowd here agreed with her.

There was something evocative about summer. Something as comfortable as a favorite pair of jeans. Or as unforgiving as walking in undersized shoes. Sandra had experienced both.

Beaver Run was beautiful in the summer, and hiking was popular, especially along the trails around the lake and the stream that fed it.

She stood behind the bar serving cold beer from the pump

and mixed drinks. Through the window, she noticed the tables outside were all occupied. Nothing else made people spend more time outside their homes than warm weather.

Miley Cyrus's "Party in the U.S.A." played in the background mixed in with the sound of conversations and clanging of cutlery.

A young couple, probably in their early twenties, got up. Or rather, the girl dragged the guy up, giggling as if someone had stuck a finger up her ass.

They turned the space between the bar area and restaurant into a dance floor. Sandra could immediately tell they were in love and that Ms. Giggly would get fucked that night. That thought again. Was she in heat?

The girl better enjoy it while it lasted, thought Sandra. It would probably be a summer she wouldn't forget fast. Sandra had once been that age and very much in love. Until the day it all ended.

To Sandra, true love was like a unicorn: much talked about and rarely seen. When it does show up, you're not so sure if what you have is the real thing.

Time would tell. But, by then, your heart would be ripped into a thousand pieces and your V card taken from you by some scoundrel.

Sandra remembered her teenage years and early twenties when she had been in love and later when the love ended. Would she ever find love again? Start a family? She wasn't getting any younger. Trevor, her brother, was hitched. She shuddered as she thought of her younger sister Alexis getting married before her. Now twenty-six, she was on a slippery slope. Her goal was to have dispensed with that by now. Would she ever trust again?

She focused on when she was in love. High school. College.

It had been magical. Then one day, it all ended.

She hummed to Miley's summer track and wondered if it had already been out that summer she'd lost her V card. No, the song that day she recalled was Will Smith's *Summertime*. The chorus to Miley's song came on. Her voice was raspy, just like Sandra's.

The door to the kitchen opened, and Laura walked in with a tray laden with food. She breezed past the bar. The smell of burgers and Cajun fries followed her like the tail of a cat. Sandra's stomach growled. She was hungry, but she'd conditioned herself to eat as little as possible when at the bar.

She nodded to the waiter standing by to let him know that the tray with the drinks was ready.

Sandra looked around at the people sitting at the bar, and they were all engrossed in their thoughts, drinks, or person they were with. Nobody needed her immediate attention.

A quick glance at the large skeleton clock on the wall reminded her it was almost time for her to call it a night. She headed to the kitchen to see how things were going there.

"Hey, Sandra," said Laura walking in behind her with her now empty tray. "A customer is going your way. He might need a ride to-"

Laura must have seen the look on Sandra's face because the words died on her lips.

Sandra took a deep breath to calm herself. *Don't say anything you would regret. Words cut deeper than the longest swords. And the wound festers.*

Even though it made good business sense to help out customers, it was her decision to make on whether to give a customer a ride or not. Sandra sighed. They'd known each other since they were kids. She had to hear Laura out first. "A customer?"

Laura put the tray down on the kitchen counter. "Yeah."

Sandra couldn't help herself. She had to say something. "Come on. I thought I was your friend. What if he's a serial killer?"

Laura shook her head. "No way. He's too good-looking to be one. Women would kill themselves for him. Heck, if I weren't already hooked, I would jerk his line."

Sandra gave her a sideways glance. "Jerk his line? In that, you're a fish, and he has a hook and line in the water?"

"Mm-hmm, something like that."

Sandra said, "I thought I was the only horny person around here tonight." She looked for the young couple, but they were nowhere to be seen.

"Well, you're not. But at least you have someone that could scratch that itch."

Sandra shot her a look. "You mean Peter? The advertising guy from Connecticut?"

Laura nodded.

"Well, Peter and I are just not clicking, and I can't wrap my fingers around what the problem is. Maybe it's because he's my dad's friend's son, I don't know. We have a date next weekend when he comes in from Connecticut."

"All right then," said Laura. "In that case, you're free. There's a customer that needs a ride."

Sandra thought for a moment. "Okay, I'll do it, but only this one time. I'll be leaving in ten minutes." Sandra paused and cocked her head. "So, who's the guy that snagged you? How come you've never mentioned him?"

"You already know, the father of my child," said Laura, brushing her black hair to the side.

Sandra knew that move. A nervous tic her friend had. Her husband, ex-husband, had been gone for three years now, and she still missed him. "I thought it was someone new." Well, she wasn't the only one thinking of lost loves. Maybe there was something in the air today.

Sandra wondered where this customer was going. There were no hotels on her way, and she knew everyone that lived in that direction. It could only be the Airbnb. "Is that another of Stone's renters?"

Lauren chuckled. "You got it."

"Okay. If I don't show up tomorrow, ask Stone about the guy that rented his house, okay?"

Laura winked. "You won't go missing, trust me." She leaned closer and whispered in her ear. "Maybe if you… emmm…let your guard down a little, you might even get your garden plowed tonight."

Sandra drew back and made a face. "What? What's with the fishing and farming euphemisms you've been spewing all night?" Sandra pointed at Laura and smiled. "I think you need to be hosed down."

Laura clapped her hands and laughed. "Touché. Now who's the queen of euphemisms? Anyway, see you later. I have a few more tables to serve before I call it quits myself. He's at table nine, position two." She winked at Sandra and turned away.

It looked like Laura knew more than she was letting on, thought Sandra. Maybe Laura was right. She did need her garden plowed.

The closest Sandra had come to come to having something with anyone was Valentine's Day when Stone's friend Mason had stopped by. She'd dropped him off at the Airbnb too. Her Valentine's date had gone south that night, and since then, she had thrown herself into her work. Running a bar was not easy.

Then Peter came along, but she just wasn't feeling him. He looked like the kind of guy that was ready to settle down, and she thought that he might grow on her. Sandra walked back to the bar from the kitchen.

She found the young couple. The guy who earlier had been reluctant to get up now had the girl pinned against the wall, his lips over her.

Sandra sighed and went behind the bar. She felt eyes on her, turned, and locked eyes with the customer sitting on her right. Sandra smiled. She was one of those biker-type females. Black leather pants and a black leather vest showing off her leather bra two sizes too small for her jugs. Sandra walked over to her and hoped she wasn't drunk, or maybe try to pick her up. It always felt awkward fighting off drunk female customers.

"What can I get you?" asked Sandra.

The lady ignored Sandra's question and said, "I heard you say you're leaving." Her voice was slurred.

"Yeah. I have to give a customer a ride."

The woman nodded. "What do you drive? A stick shift?"

Sandra knew where she was going with that questioning. "Yes, and it gets me wherever I want to go."

Ms. All Leather pursed her lips. "Is that right? You know, if you hitch a ride on my face, you'll get there faster. I guarantee that." She leaned closer. "And it doesn't need refueling, like your stick shift to get you there again."

Heat rushed to Sandra's cheeks. She didn't want to start that conversation either. "Sorry, I really need to go." As she walked away, she said, "And I love my stick shift."

Sandra went to the bathroom and freshened up. Laura had told her the table number so she knew where to look. His frame looked familiar as she approached. "No...it can't be," she whispered to herself. Stone would have mentioned it. Then she remembered Stone was new to Beaver Run. He wouldn't have known him.

The man tapped away on his phone screen.

Sandra stopped in her tracks.

Her pulse raced. The music disappeared, then reappeared. Her heartbeat relocated to her head as loud drums. She recognized that frame. He had filled out more, but she knew it well. After all these years and thinking about him barely an hour ago, there he was.

Now everything made sense. The way Laura had been talking about getting hooked like a fish and plowing gardens.

Sandra stood there like a deer caught in car headlights. Long enough for that sixth sense people have when someone was looking at them to kick in. The man looked up, and their eyes locked.

The man squinted, then his eyebrows shot up. His mouth widened in a grin.

4

Sandra

ONCE THEIR EYES MET, AND HE'D RECOGNIZED HER, HEAT engulfed her. A tingle traveled down her spine, spread out over her butt, and settled between her legs. God, she still had the hots for that piece of shit. His smiling face drew her back to a time so many years ago when that smile was for her alone. It brightened her day and made her moist between the legs.

She breathed out his name after he called hers. Her whole body turned into one giant heartbeat. She watched his eyes move from her head, down her little sundress to her cowboy boots, and back to her shocked face.

The glint was there-he'd literally eye-fucked her. He wanted her just like old times. *Jesus.* A fuzzy feeling started from her stomach and dispersed heat all over her body. Sandra was surprised by her own reaction. She wanted him too. Was it because she hadn't had her garden tended to in a *long* time?

Luke sprang to his feet and started toward her. He'd filled out more. His black hair looked like he'd just rolled out of bed. A two- or three-day stubble gave him an edgy look. The black T-shirt hugged his body like a second skin, showing bulges where it mattered. Evidence that he gave a premium to fitness. Probably visited the gym or did some type of virtual workout.

Then the cobwebs clouding her senses fell apart. She was back in the present: the music, people's conversations, the sound of cutlery on plates. The smell of beer, fried food, coffee, and something that reminded her of sex all rushed through her.

The closer he got, the more overheated she felt. Could she handle this? Laura should have warned her. Laura had set her up. She knew Luke was out there.

Sandra couldn't wait to get her hands around Laura's neck.

A jolt of abject terror and want shot through her. Had he come back for her after all these years? Was he here to continue from where they'd stopped?

Sandra considered turning around and running, but he was already upon her. His hands, huge artist's hands, spread out in front of him like the wings of a wandering albatross. *Spread out? Lady! Again, get your mind out of the gutter.* But those fingers that made fantastic art had also created out of this world sensations between her legs.

"Sandra!" He engulfed her in a bear hug.

The faint smell of cologne, stale sweat, and him engulfed her. She sank into him like a missing puzzle piece pushed into the right spot. For one brief moment, Sandra was transported to when they were teenagers and doing each other all over town in the back of his truck.

He drew back and looked at her again. "You look great!"

He pulled her into his arms once more and squeezed. Then he stepped back. "What are you doing here?"

Sandra smiled. "What do you mean? I live here. The question should be, what are you doing here?"

Luke chuckled. "I'm from here too. Born and bred." He pointed at her. "Wait, are you my ride? Laura told me a colleague of hers was going my way."

Sandra nodded and looked around. She bet Laura was somewhere laughing her head off enjoying the little collision she'd engineered.

More people stood and rocked to music even though it was not a dance floor. Summer could do that to you. But nobody paid any attention to them, which was good.

Sandra cocked her head toward the door. "Come, it's a bit noisy. Let's step outside."

"Okay."

She led the way, and Luke followed. She felt heat on her back and was sure his eyes were glued to her ass.

The air outside was warmer, typical July weather. But it felt better, probably because there was more of it.

They stood at the side porch of the restaurant. Not far from them, moonlight glistened off the surface of Beaver Run Lake, giving off a romantic vibe.

Sandra turned and faced him. "So what brings you back?"

"Beaver Run has some amazing landscapes. I came to paint." He shrugged. "Work."

A brief pang of disappointment seared through her heart. Even though it was a shot in the dark, she'd hoped he came back to find her. Sandra nodded, shaking the regret off as she brushed her hair behind her ears. "The art. How's it going?"

"Not bad. I've been all over the country painting landscapes. I just came from Minnesota-Jersey's my last stop."

Luke exhaled. "What about you? I have to tell you, Sandra, you look as gorgeous as ever. Good enough to be eaten."

Sandra rolled her eyes. *Well, if I look that good, why did you walk out on me?* But she didn't say that. Instead, she said, "I'm fine. Worked at a bar in New York for a year. I was always coming back to Beaver Run to see Mom and Dad. And-"

"Yes, your parents. How are they? Such nice people."

"Getting on, like everybody else. Sorry about your loss. I heard about your father. I thought you would have come back then."

"Thanks. By the time I got the news and made it down to the nursing home, he'd already been buried. My dad's will said he wanted to be buried right away next to my mother. He bought the two plots together at the cemetery between Beaver Run and Mountain Peak." Luke sighed and stared ahead.

Sandra wanted to say something but couldn't think of the right thing to say.

Luke shrugged. "Dad was a loner. Most of his friends were already gone. The house was sold ages ago for medical bills, so there was really nothing to come back to Beaver Run for." His eyes bore into hers. "Anyway, let's stop talking about deaths." Luke smiled. "You look gorgeous. So how come you work in a bar now? I didn't see that coming."

Sandra laughed. "Part owner." Enjoying the compliment.

"Owner? Wow!"

She looked around and motioned at a passing waiter.

"Hi Sandra, what can I get you?" asked the waiter, holding out a pad and pen.

She looked at Luke, palm raised. "Wait, let me guess, Coke and Hennessey?"

Luke nodded. "And yours is…can you drink on the job?"

"I've clocked out."

"Okay, orange juice and vodka then," said Luke looking at the waiter.

She smiled and nodded.

The waiter put away his pad. "I'll be right back."

"To answer your question, I worked in a bar and was visiting Beaver Run all the time. When Mr. Taylor decided to retire and put the bar up for sale, I thought, *Why not?* It's a partnership, though. What about you? You're so talented. How's the creative life treating you?"

Luke inhaled and let out a sigh. "Well, not bad. Still working on it."

"Okay," said Sandra. She noticed his reluctance and made a mental note to remind herself not to bring up how he was doing again. It was a loaded topic. Their drinks arrived. She picked up her glass. "Cheers."

"Cheers," said Luke and picked up his glass.

She stared into the parking lot. "What happened to your ride?"

Luke pursed his lips. "The Cherokee just gave up the ghost. I'll find out exactly what happened when I get someone to look at it. I guess it's better it died in your parking lot than on the highway."

"True. Otherwise, you would've been stuck on some highway waiting for Triple-A with mountain lions checking you out."

"Mountain lions in New Jersey?" asked Luke.

"Of course. They're everywhere. You would have also missed out on the pleasure of dipping into our Cajun delight." Her voice took on a low deep tone. Sandra couldn't believe she was flirting with him after what he did to her.

"Oh, those fries were gorgeous. Just like you."

"Really?" She'd wanted to pretend she didn't hear that, but she also wanted to explore that train of thought. "How would you know that? It's been such a long time." He was her first love. She'd given him her V card in the back seat of his truck, and after that, they'd done it all over town. Anywhere they found privacy.

Luke pursed his lips and raised an eyebrow. "How would I know?"

Sandra nodded. They'd gone to Rutgers, and when Luke graduated, he decided he needed to go off on his own. Over the years, she'd dated a few guys, just for sex, the release. But none had compared to him. She wouldn't mind having him. It had been a long time. She looked at his lips and imagined them between her legs, speaking to her garden. A shudder ran through her.

Luke twirled his glass then tossed what was left down his throat. "So are you seeing anyone?"

Sandra copied him, then chuckled. "So...asks the guy that told me we had to move on." She eyed his glass. "Do you want another drink? I'm driving, and one is my limit."

Luke fiddled with his now empty glass. "No, I'm good."

"So...you're trying to arrange a booty call for when you're in Beaver Run?"

Luke inhaled nosily and drew back.

Sandra saw the desire in his eyes. He would bend her over the table and take her right here if she said the word. The power she had over him excited her. Who knows, he might still get lucky. "You seem very sure of yourself. Like if I'm not seeing anyone, then I'm available for you, just like that." She snapped her fingers. "You think Okafor's Law is going to work on me?"

Luke's eyes narrowed-he cocked his head. "Okafor's Law? What's that?"

She leaned close to him and cooed in her sexiest voice. "Once you've fucked a girl and done a good job of it, you can come back anytime, and she will indulge you. Basically, you've earned a get into her panties key. Like the get out of jail card in Monopoly."

"What the…Really?" said Luke, grinning from ear to ear. "Tell me more."

"Anyway, I'm ready to go. It's been a long day." She headed for the stairs that led to the parking lot, andLuke followed. "Is there anything you need to grab from your car?"

"Yes, just a few things."

"Okay, I'll go get my car and pull up beside you," said Sandra and walked over to back where her Ford was parked. There was a spring to her step. The sparks were really flying between them after all these years.

Luke stood beside his car with a large canvas bag and a small suitcase with wheels when she pulled up.

He opened the back passenger side door. "Nice truck." He put his stuff in the back and shut the door. Then he opened the front passenger side and stepped in.

Sandra's dress had ridden up her thighs when she'd gotten in, and she'd conveniently forgotten to pull it down. The car's interior lights came on when he opened the door, and she was pleased when his eyes roamed over her thighs.

"It's not far, right?" asked Luke.

Sandra's girly bits twitched with anticipation. "Nope." She stepped on the gas.

5

Luke

LUKE SAT IN SANDRA'S TRUCK AND JUST COULDN'T BELIEVE what had just happened. Of all the eating places in New Jersey, his vehicle had picked his ex-girlfriend's restaurant.

Providence?

He was sure if he looked up the hand of God in the dictionary, there would be a picture of Beaver Tail Bar and Restaurant right there. To make things worse, Sandra looked so good he wondered what had possessed him four years ago to walk away from her.

Since then, he'd developed a tendency to walk away from people. Pack and relocate once people started to get comfortable with him. He never got involved with women long enough for a serious relationship. Sex was a release for him. Now, Sandra had brought up Okafor's Law. Did he have a chance? Or was she just teasing? His cock jumped. Time would tell.

Luke looked out of the car's window to keep his mind

away from what he would like to do to her. They drove past The Glass Flower shop and the elementary, middle, and high school building, landmarks he remembered. They had all gone there. Not far away from there was the rec center where he'd worked as a lifeguard for several summers. Then the library and then the sheriff's office. Beaver Run hadn't changed much.

"It seems like Trevor is in tonight," said Sandra, looking at the sheriff's office.

"Trevor...?"

"My brother Trevor. You remember him, don't you?"

"Of course, I remember him." He had been two years ahead of them in high school. They were not friends, but it was such a small town that everybody knew everyone else. Then there are people you hang out with who are your buddies. Trevor was cool. "He's in law enforcement? He struck me more as the military type."

"Deputy sheriff. But he was in the army. Now he's keeping the town safe. Stone, the guy you rented the house from, is his buddy."

"Hmmm, I don't remember him."

"He didn't grow up here. He moved here for work."

"I thought people were moving out," said Luke. "Looking for something bigger and better."

Sandra cocked her head and nodded. "You're right, but some found their way back somehow. I'm back—Trevor's back, Laura never left. I'm sure others will one day come back. Aging parents, nostalgia...you just arrived. The question now is, are you here for good?"

Luke laughed. "I think I have wanderlust."

"An irresistible urge that makes you grab your bag and take off," said Sandra. "I have firsthand knowledge of that. I wonder if it has a cure?"

Luke wanted to tell her how sorry he was, but he didn't want to reopen old wounds. She seemed to have recovered from the breakup. *You ditched her…it was no breakup.*

His eyes kept on drifting to her thighs as if he had night goggles on. How he would love to see what was farther upstream.

An intense desire to spread her out on a bed and take his time with her seized him. He would massage her. Work his way up-toes, feet, calves, thighs, and the wonderful garden between her legs. Luke's jeans tightened.

He would lower his head, taste her saltness. Slip one finger, then two, into her wetness. Stroke the roof of her pussy, strong side-to-side strokes as fast he could, with his lips fastened on her clit.

She would grab his head and try to shove his face into her. Writhe on the bed, her thighs squeezing and releasing his head sandwiched between them. He wouldn't relent on his actions until she screamed his name and coated his tongue with her cum.

"Earth to Luke. What's on your mind?"

"Sorry. I was just thinking about old times."

"That's good."

Luke expected her to say more, but she didn't.

Moments later, Sandra turned into a driveway with a ranch-style building. "We're here. Did he tell you where to find the key?"

Luke raised his cell phone. "I think so." He tapped the screen with his finger. After a few more taps and slides, he said, "The key is in a flowerpot gargoyle."

Sandra groaned and turned off the car. "Come on, I'll show you where it is." She opened the door and stepped out. "The last guy I brought here was lucky I didn't just drop him and drive away. He didn't even know what a gargoyle looked like."

Luke clenched his jaw. "You've brought men here before?"

Sandra glanced at him, an amused look on her face. "Jealous are we? Yeah, a few times."

A light came on as they approached the door.

Sandra stopped and looked at the light. "Motion-activated. That's new." She stooped and retrieved the key from under the pot in the image of an ugly man with horns and wings. She held out the key. "Do you need help moving your stuff?"

"No. I've got it. But you can come in to make sure I settle in."

Sandra smiled and unlocked the door.

Luke came up behind her. The security light in front of her made her dress see-through. He could see the outline of her underwear. What color was it?

Once inside, Sandra turned on the lights as she walked toward the kitchen. She opened the refrigerator and looked inside. "You'll have to stock it up with things you like to eat."

Luke put down his bags and went to the kitchen. "What's in there?" He peered over her shoulder and inhaled. A clean, flowery scent wafted up to his nose.

Sandra spun around. "There's-"

His face was directly opposite hers. Time froze, and for a few seconds, they stood there trading air.

Her lips parted, and she placed a palm on his chest.

Luke expected her to push, but she didn't. He placed his palms on her side, slid down, and circled to her back. He pulled her toward his body, his erection brushed against her, and he cupped her ass.

A sexy gasp escaped Sandra's lips. Her breath was hot on his face.

"I've been hard for you since I saw you in your bar. I didn't know what you meant to me until this night." His hands ran up and down her body, and he felt her tremble. Luke planted a kiss between her neck and shoulder.

She stretched her neck to the side, giving him more room, and he obliged her, running wet kisses up and down her neck.

It was like they were doing a choreographed dance, picking up from where they'd stopped four years ago. Luke's heart was pounding, his cock straining to explode out of his jeans. He remembered his thoughts earlier, spreading her out and eating her pussy until she came on his lips. He really wanted to do that.

Tiny moans escaped from her throat.

Luke pulled back and watched her mouth. He took her lips. His own body sizzled like hot coals splashed with water. Their lips were glued together like opposite ends of a magnet.

She was nibbling, biting, thrusting her tongue in and out of his mouth. She pushed her body against his, grinding on his cock.

Luke lowered his hands and slipped them under her dress, up her to her hips. He groaned as he felt the coolness of her skin against his palms. He moved his hand to the front and reached for her crotch. Her panties were completely soaked.

Sandra gasped. "Luke." Her voice was low and sexy.

His whole body was on fire. He dipped his fingers underneath the bands of Sandra's panties and was inside.

Luke let out a shaky breath and ran his thumb over the tuft of coarse hair between her legs, stroking her pussy lips. "So wet."

"It's all your doing," said Sandra in a tight sexy voice.

Luke agreed and took it as an invitation to continue to plunder her privates with his fingers. "Do you like?"

She leaned into him, moaning and rocking her hips against his hands. "Yes...love it...feels so good." Her voice was sexy, the words barely audible.

He stroked her clit, exploring her wetness. Slowly he slipped a finger into her core. "You drive me crazy, Sandra. I've never wanted anyone as much as I want you right now."

"I want you too." She rocked her hips against his fingers, looking for the right position for maximum pleasure.

"I'm so glad we reconnected," said Luke, his voice tight and full of want.

She wriggled her hips, faster and faster. Seeking more friction, more pleasure. "Same here."

"I fought hard to resist you," said Luke. "But I lost the battle." He worked his fingers faster and faster. What he wanted to do now was whip out his cock, bend her over, and slide into her wet pussy.

Sandra moaned. "Don't stop."

Her moans urged him on. She was climbing that proverbial hill. He was going to get her there and launch her into the stratosphere. Then he would spread her out and plunge his cock into her tight warm pussy.

They were almost inside the refrigerator. The contents rattled violently as he stroked, and she rocked her hips to meet his fingers.

Sandra moaned. "I'm almost there...I...I'm almost there." She was breathless. "Make me come, Luke."

Luke nestled his face between the crook of her neck. The sound of her voice and her plea almost made him lose control. "My pleasure," said Luke, his words muffled against her neck. He slipped a third finger into her, the whole ensemble curved upwards. He stroked faster.

Her breathing came in open-mouthed gasps.

Luke didn't stop.

Then Sandra let out a scream as she came undone. She moaned and said his name over and over again. She placed her palm on his shoulder to steady herself, gasping as she sucked in air. "Oh my God, oh my God." She shuddered as if ice cubes had been thrown down her dress.

Luke gazed into her eyes and smiled. She had that glassy look which was very satisfying to him. He'd done his job. "Sandra, do you want to take this to the couch, so you can get on top?" Then her phone started to ring.

Sandra's head whirled from side to side. "Where is my phone?" She saw it on the kitchen island and walked over to pick it up.

"Don't answer it," said Luke.

"I have to. It's the restaurant. It could be important." She raised the phone to her ear. "Hello." Sandra listened, inhaling and exhaling. Her breathing coming back to normal. "Okay, I'll be there." She turned to Luke. "I have to go."

"W…what?"

She headed for the door, turned, and smiled. "Thank you. I'll stop by in the morning to see if you need a ride…to the bar."

Luke groaned. "What about…?" He pointed at his crotch.

"Bye." She stepped out of the door.

Luke watched her drive away. He stood there until the sound of her car engine dwindled to nothing, replaced by the sound of crickets.

He couldn't understand why she'd left. His cock was about to rupture.

Luke shut and locked the main door. Then he explored the rest of the house, sniffing his fingers as he went, envious of them. They'd been where he desperately wanted to be.

He opened a door. It was a closet with a washer and dryer stacked up together.

The next door was a half bathroom. Luke let out a sigh. She'd left him no choice. He dropped his jeans and boxers, setting his cock free.

The sound of her moans rang in his ears. This was wrong, so wrong. He imagined Sandra spread out on the kitchen island. His cock replaced his fingers, massaging her pussy lips and clit, then sliding into her.

That image sent a shot of desire through him. He grabbed his swollen cock and stroked hard.

Sandra Leigh, the sexy girl that had worshiped the ground he walked on, whom he had unceremoniously sent packing, had completely taken over his mind. He was inside her, pumping in and out. Her smell on his nostrils was like throwing gasoline on a fire. It drove his hand to stroke faster.

He reached the point of no return. "Fuck." He sounded raspy, nothing like him. His orgasm, like thick ropes shot out of him, landed in the bowl and sank to the bottom. "Goodness." He couldn't believe how fast and hard he came.

Luke took long deep breaths, grabbed a handful of tissue, cleaned up, tossed it into the water, and flushed.

He pulled up his boxers and jeans and headed for the bedroom. All of a sudden, the fatigue of the whole day descended on him.

His mind went to work on how to get his cock into Sandra's panties. As a plan took form, sleep took him. Tomorrow…

6

Sandra

THE ALARM ON SANDRA'S PHONE WENT OFF, AND SHE KNEW it was 6:30 a.m. She groaned and swept her hand across the bedsheet until she found her phone. She looked at the screen and hit snooze.

She tried to continue with sleep but never made it back to that REM cycle sleep experts say is good for you. Sandra still couldn't understand why a part of the sleep cycle called Rapid Eye Movement could be good for you. Didn't the rapid in it stand for anything?

Her and her foolish musing. She would have to drag herself out of bed and get ready for her run. Compared to REM, you don't run a trail with your eyes closed. She pondered whether to skip going for a run this morning and swim at night at the rec center. With her premium membership, she had unlimited access, day or night. Then she remembered she had to be at the bar for closing.

Her alarm went off again. "Okay, time to get up. One, two three…four, five, six go!" Sandra didn't move. She better stop counting. Where was Mel Robbins and her five-second rule when you needed her? Then her snooze went off again, and that was when she rolled out of bed.

Sandra went to the bathroom, peed, brushed her teeth, and slipped into her running outfit. Within minutes she was out of the door and headed to the trail close to her house.

The sun was up, and the air smelled of freshly cut grass. It seemed like one of her neighbors had already mown their lawn this early.

She lived on a short, quiet street where the homes were primarily two- to three-bedroom houses. Hers was a three bedroom, and she used the third room as a study.

She had her Bluetooth Airpods clipped over her ears, her iPhone in an armband on her left bicep, and off she went.

Sandra listened to the audiobook *Pride and Prejudice* as she ran. Or tried to listen to it. Her thoughts were filled with Luke and what had happened last night. She'd hoped the audiobook and the exercise would take her mind off him, but it didn't.

It was like he had her pleasure blueprint in his hands. No wonder she'd always used him as a yardstick to measure the few guys she'd been with after him. They all paled compared to that performance last night.

Why did he even come back here? There were other places he could have gone to paint.

Anger flashed through her at the thought of him treating her as just a warm body. She was glad she hadn't fucked him. It was a close call, though.

Her anger dissipated just as it started. She was angry with Luke for what he did in the past, abandoning her. She knew him. Luke wasn't into taking advantage of people. What happened last night was a spur-of-the-moment thing. Two people that used to be intimate suddenly found themselves alone after so many years of separation.

Sandra chuckled. That must be Okafor's Law in play.

They hadn't really broken up as enemies. Just that she still didn't understand what had happened four years ago at college. Why he decided to leave.

Sandra got off the track to make way for a couple riding bicycles coming toward her. She smiled at them, and after they passed, continued. She would run to the boundary where the trail entered the forest, and on her way back, would speed walk.

The last five minutes of her run was usually a cool-down session. Better for her to be back to normal by the time she got into the shower. Sandra hated coming out of the bathroom with sweat still pouring out of her pores.

Once back home, she headed to the kitchen, put fresh water in her coffee maker, and turned it on.

In the bathroom, she peeled off her sweaty outfit and got in the shower.

Ten minutes later, Sandra was in the kitchen dressed in a white blouse over faded blue jeans. She pushed the button on the coffee maker, and as it gurgled and sucked in water, she heard the sound of an incoming text.

The text was from her mother and said, *Stop by on your way*. What did she want now? Maybe she'd unplugged her computer or cable while vacuuming, and *Now the darn machine isn't coming on,* she imagined her mother saying.

The coffee maker spluttered, and the black liquid trickled down into her to-go cup, filling her kitchen with the aroma of French vanilla.

Sandra tapped the screen to speed-dial her mother and find out what she wanted. She stopped. She would drop by instead.

As her garage door opened and she backed out of her driveway, Sandra contemplated stopping at the Airbnb first, then changed her mind. She didn't want to appear too eager.

"So, what happened at the bar last night?" asked her mother as she unpacked groceries from the kitchen counter and stocked the fridge.

Sandra knew something was up. This was the second time her mother had asked the question after letting her in about five minutes ago. The first time she'd pretended she didn't hear the question.

Her mother stared at her. "Are you all right?"

"Okay, Mother, spill it. I know you were at the grocery store. You must have heard more than the usual 'Clean up on aisle 6' over the loudspeaker."

"That's the bread aisle, dear. The only thing customers knock over there is bread, and it doesn't make a mess."

Sandra let out an exasperated groan and started unloading a bag. "Come on, Mom." She unpacked cans of soup and stewed tomatoes and walked toward the cabinet for soup cans. The arrangement remained the same as when they were kids and lived in the house.

"Okay, Okay. I saw the librarian, and somehow we got talking about the late Mr. Martin…"

"The librarian? That's Laura's mom. You make it sound like something official that had to do with books and the library."

"Fine. I saw Sally, and she said Laura told her that a certain Luke Martin was back in town and that you two took off together last night." She looked at the clock in the kitchen.

"And you're a bit late today. Did he spend the night at your place?"

Heat rushed to Sandra's cheeks. Thank God her mother wasn't looking. She would have seen her change color like a chameleon. Her mother was close with her deduction.

"No, Mother! I hit the snooze button several times, then went for a run. Laura must have forgotten to mention that his car had broken down at the bar, and she suggested I gave him a ride. He's staying at Stone's place."

"All right, all right. Don't bite my head off. I was just hoping he came back for you. You guys looked great together."

"That was a long time ago, Mother."

Footsteps pounded down the stairs.

"Hi Sandra," said their dad as he walked into the kitchen. "How are you?"

Sandra was happy to see her father. She smiled. "Morning, Dad. How are you?"

"Couldn't be better. I heard you guys from upstairs. In the weeds already? What happened at the bar last night? I hope it wasn't a fight. Better let Trevor know. At least that's his department."

Sandra let out an exasperated breath. Not her father too.

"Your mother and Sally were in deep conversation at the grocery store," said her father. "They held up our shopping for a few minutes. Instead of loading the cart, I stood sentry. I couldn't help but hear bits and pieces of their discussion."

Sandra didn't want to hear more. Seeing how her father was dressed gave her an idea to change the subject. "Are you going fishing?"

Dad nodded. "Going to the lake. The other side of the lake with the hanging bridge. Away from the bar, tourists and what have you."

Sandra raised an eyebrow. "Are you saying that my restaurant is noisy?"

"No," said Mom. "He's just saying that a girl has no business running a bar and should be pinning down a man."

Dad raised his hand and turned to Mother, then to Sandra. "Ladies, I can speak for myself, thank you. Right now, I'm going fishing, where it's a lot quieter."

Her father was a retired foreman in a rivet factory in Morristown. Her mother had stayed home to raise her and her brother and sister. They were both in their sixties now and had a little extra time on their hands.

As Laura drove to meet up with Luke, she tried to put the altercation behind her. Mother always stuck her nose into other people's business. One of these days, she would get it chopped off.

Sandra wanted to call Luke and let him know she was on her way and was tickled she didn't have his number. She'd let him finger fuck her but didn't even have his phone number. She smiled as she remembered last night and the look on his face when she left.

Minutes later, she arrived at his place.

Sandra stood by the door after she'd rung the bell for the third time. She knew Luke wasn't a deep sleeper unless he was exhausted. Could he have changed in the past few years? Or did something happen to him? Her pulse sped up.

She raised her hand to bang on the door when she heard faint footsteps behind her. She cocked her head. Yes, those were footsteps, and they were coming fast behind her. She whirled around.

Behind her was Luke, dressed in shorts, sneakers, and nothing else. Sweat poured down his torso, turning his shorts into an overwhelmed sponge. His muscles stood tense and taut.

She should have known. Sandra let out a breath. After all, it was he that had introduced her to running. She remembered when they would have grungy, energy-filled sex after a run.

"Hi," said Sandra, her voice hoarse, eyes fixed on his six-pack.

7

Luke

LUKE WAS AWAKE ONCE DAYLIGHT STREAMED IN THROUGH THE windows around 4:30 am. He stayed in bed for an hour with thoughts about Sandra on his mind. In his wildest fantasies, he couldn't have dreamed up his car would break down close to Sandra's restaurant, and she would end up dropping him off.

He got out of bed and explored his surroundings. From his experience, things seen at night for the first time always looked different during the day. He liked the house. He could tell a lot of thought had been put into the decorations, mostly high-end.

Luke walked over to the fridge and noticed a magnetic picture frame of a couple on the door. Probably the owner. The woman with him looked familiar. Someone from his school?

Luke smiled as he pulled the door open, remembering

what had taken place right there last night. If furniture and appliances could speak, they would have a lot to say.

Thirsty, Luke grabbed an eight-ounce bottle of water and chugged it. The water cooled his insides as it traveled down. He should have made arrangements with Sandra to pick him up on her way to the bar. He hadn't asked her to stop by, but knowing her, she would.

Luke groaned when he remembered his car. He would have to fix it, otherwise getting around would be tough. He tossed the empty bottle into the trash, paused, and took it out.

He went through the cabinets and found an empty grocery plastic bag. He tossed the empty bottle into it. That would be his recycling garbage bag.

Luke walked over to where he'd dropped his bags. The large canvas bag contained his paintings. A traveling bag had his clothes, and a messenger bag had things like his passport, checkbooks, and other paper odds and ends. His running shoes were still in the car. He would just run with the sneakers he had on.

He knew the area and decided how far he would run. He contemplated leaving a note for Sandra. He knew he would struggle with what to write. He might end up with something inappropriate, and what if somebody else saw it? He scrapped the idea.

Luke made a right, started a slow jog, then picked up pace. Would people still recognize him? Maybe. He wondered if, in the next few minutes, a police car would pull up behind him, called in by a homeowner about a suspicious character.

Luke focused on his run. The plan wasn't to exhaust himself, just to get his blood flowing and his heart pumping to get him ready for the day. He ran up to the junction that led to the main road to the center of town, then turned around.

Coming back was faster, and every truck he saw looked like Sandra's F-150. His plan for the day was taking shape in his head, but he would need Sandra's help.

Get the mechanic to look at the Cherokee. And while he was doing that, grab a ride with Sandra to the woods to find a suitable location for his painting.

Hopefully, his car would be ready by evening.

Once the Airbnb came into view, he reduced his speed, then walked the rest of the way.

Panting, he turned into his driveway, and there was Sandra about to knock on the door. She looked dashing in a white blouse and jeans, as beautiful as ever.

She turned around to the sound of his feet and smiled. Her eyes traveled up and down his body.

Luke saw the way her eyes were glued to his shorts and knew all wasn't lost. He grinned. "Thanks so much for stopping by. I was going to walk to the bar after getting ready."

Sandra chuckled. "I can see you still run."

"Nothing jumpstarts your day like a good run."

The distance to the bar always looks short," said Sandra, "but it's quite a long walk. I thought you might need a ride."

Luke reached for the doorknob and turned it. "Thanks again for coming. Quick question. Is there any mechanic you know I could get to look at my car?" He opened the door and held it as she walked in. "You can hold your breath. I know I stink." But he did the opposite and inhaled as she passed. "You smell nice."

Color rushed to Sandra's cheeks. "Thank you."

"Make yourself at home. I'll be in and out of the shower before you know it." Luke grabbed his suitcase with his clothes and disappeared into the bedroom.

Just like he'd promised, he was in and out as fast as he

could. He walked back to the living room, pulling his T-shirt over his head.

"That was fast," said Sandra, sitting on the edge of the couch, holding a computer magazine in her hand. "I see you still keep in shape."

Luke adjusted his shoulders and noticed the twinkle again in her eyes. "I have to. Otherwise, pretty ladies like you won't take a second look at me."

Sandra smiled and looked away, shaking her head.

"You totally occupied my mind last night, then you left me stranded." As soon as the words left Luke's mouth, he knew it was the wrong choice of words.

Sandra's head shot up. "Well, you should know about leaving people stranded."

Luke felt like he'd been punched in the stomach. "Sorry."

"That was four years ago. I've grown some scar tissue over the wound." She walked closer to him.

Sandra was so close that he could smell her flowery shampoo.

"I didn't mean to say that." What was on his mind was that he wanted to bury his cock inside her so badly, and he knew she wanted him too. He raised his hand in an *I surrender* gesture. "I didn't come here with any ulterior motives. My car breaking down and me ending up in your bar wasn't planned."

Sandra gave a non-committal nod.

"I have a commission to create some artwork. I know the landscape here well, just like you." He chuckled. "We spent a lot of time in those woods together. I knew it would serve my purpose." Luke pursed his lips. "I do think of those times. Leaving you at college wasn't right. I own up to that. But sometimes…"

Sandra agreed with him, nodding her head.

"Who would have guessed that you would own a bar?"

Sandra said, "Listen Luke, I don't think you're a bad guy, but like you said, you just like to get up and go. You've been on my mind continuously over the years. I just came from my parents' home. Can you guess what we talked about?"

Luke shook his head. His pulse started to race. "What?"

"You."

Luke slammed his palm against his chest. "Me?"

"You were the topic. Word has already gotten around that you're back, and the two of us were seen together."

"But you only gave me a ride because my car was broken."

"That's true, but that fact seemed to have been omitted. They remember us as we were during and after high school, in love and inseparable. They didn't see the college years, which was equally good until it wasn't. You left."

Luke wanted to say he was sorry again, but he didn't want to sound like a broken record.

"I didn't know I still had such feelings for you. There's nothing I would have loved more than to lay you down on that couch, mount you, and ride you until you were screaming my name."

Luke's breath hitched. He cocked his head. "What did you say?" His cock started to get hard.

"You heard correctly. I would've had sex with you."

The confines of Luke's boxers suddenly felt too small.

"I'm twenty-six now. Twenty-eight, thirty is not far away. I thought you were the one before. But you woke up one morning unprovoked and decided you were moving on. There's no guarantee it won't happen again. I can't afford to invest time into something that could go nowhere."

Luke just stared at her. She was right in so many ways. He had to be careful with what he said when he did speak.

"It wasn't easy for me either. Actually, it was your car that stopped me from fucking you."

His cock was already losing steam, but when she said fuck, it went back to steel. "How…how did my car do that?"

"It was one of my workers on the phone. Wanted to confirm I knew about the car left in the parking lot or call the police."

"Sandra, I can't apologize enough for what happened in college. I still don't know…" His voice trailed off.

"That's exactly what I'm saying. I can ignore the past and say I want us to continue where we left off. I'm a big girl. I can handle it. Whatever I decide to do, I keep an eye on the future. I know you'll finish your painting and move on."

He had no comeback to that. That had been his plan until his car broke down.

"Come on, let's go. You haven't even been here for twenty-four hours, and things are getting too serious."

Luke put on his shoes and followed her out.

"You're not bringing anything?" asked Sandra.

"Most of my tools are in my car." He locked the door and got in the car. "Do you have any mechanic in mind?" He felt it was better they changed the topic. It wasn't going his way at all. They were digging up things that were better left buried.

8

Sandra

SANDRA BACKED INTO THE ROAD, PUT THE CAR IN DRIVE, AND headed toward Main Street. She was not a mean person, just that Luke made her spell it out to him.

The faint smell of his cologne-aromatic, fresh, masculine with a dash of citrus reminded her of old times.

Feeling bad for how she'd spoken earlier, she stole a quick glance at him. His face was passive, staring ahead.

"We'll stop at Moe's Garage," said Sandra. "He's reliable. They might be busy, but at least they can come to the bar to check out your car at their convenience."

Luke looked around. "That would be great. I ran on this road this morning. It hasn't changed much."

"Did you see anyone?"

Luke laughed. "A few people."

She stole another look at him. His dimpled cheeks and the way his lips crinkled reminded her of the things she liked about him.

"You mean people I know. It's been such a long time, but I'm sure I'll recognize some of the town folks in due course, and they, me."

They drove in silence.

Luke turned to her. "How's your sister Alexis? Is she in Beaver Run?"

Sandra felt a tightness in her chest. Why was he asking about Alexis? "She's fine. Went to Europe for the summer. Why are you asking?"

"I knew someone in your family hasn't been accounted for, so I was trying to figure out who." Luke looked at her. "Which countries is she visiting? Let me guess-England, France, Germany."

Sandra pushed the turn signal, and a faint click, click, click sound came on. "Yeah, plus Spain and some other ones." She turned into a coffee shop.

"I'm sure you must be hungry."

"That's an understatement. I'm famished. Since I left your restaurant last night, I haven't eaten. The kitchen in the house was well stocked, but I wasn't expecting you. Well…I hoped you would come. I was going to make something to eat after running." He looked at the coffee shop. "This looks more promising."

"Mrs. Miller runs it now. You'll like it. They make the best sausage, egg, and cheese croissant sandwich in New Jersey."

"I'll have that then."

The smell of coffee and something baking in the oven wafted in the air. In a display behind the cashier was an assortment of donuts, muffins, and other baked goods.

Sandra ordered an English muffin with egg, and a cup of coffee, and the croissant sandwich for Luke.

"I'm watching my weight," she said before Luke could

complain she wasn't eating the best sandwich in New Jersey she'd recommended.

"But you don't need to watch anything. I'm already watching you."

Sandra did a slight head shake and smiled. "Foolish." Her eyebrows shot up. "Do you want to eat here or take it to go?"

"It's your call. You're driving. I can eat anywhere."

A few minutes later, the cashier called their order.

"Hi, Sandra."

Sandra smiled at her and reached into her handbag. "Good morning, Megan."

Megan spoke slowly as if distracted. "The donuts are not ready yet."

Sandra shook her head. "No, that's fine. I just came to get breakfast. You can have them delivered to the restaurant as usual. Forget I was here."

Megan's eyes narrowed, and she pointed at him. "You look familiar. Is that Luke Martin from a hundred years ago?"

Luke grinned. "Hello, Mrs. Miller, good to see you."

Megan beamed. "Good to see you too! Wow, just like old times. You two are back together already?"

Luke and Sandra said no at the same time.

"No! He's here for work," said Sandra. Now she was really glad nothing had happened last night. He'd said no so eagerly.

"I paint landscapes, and my car broke down at the restaurant last night…it's a long story."

"I bet it is," said Megan. "Those landscapes take a while to paint, so I guess I'll see you again."

"I guess so," said Luke. "Nice seeing you again." He collected his sandwich and stepped out of the line.

Sandra's muffin was already unwrapped, and she ate as they headed toward the car. By the time they got to it, she crumpled the wrapper into a ball and tossed it into the garbage. "We'll stop at Moe's and take it from there." She took a sip of coffee. "I don't know why bought coffee always tastes different from the one you make at home. Even if it's the same brand and type."

"Good point," said Luke as he got into the passenger side. "I don't know why either."

Half a block later, Sandra turned onto a mechanic's garage. "This is Moe's." She pulled into a parking spot and killed the engine. "Come on."

Luke stuffed the rest of his sandwich into his mouth and took a sip of coffee. He placed the cup back in the cup holder and came out of the car, still chewing. He followed Sandra as she headed toward the office. A bell dinged as a car drove into the garage.

Sandra pushed the door, and they stepped in. It was a regular mechanic waiting room-a counter, a table with magazines and newspapers spread out on it, and two chairs.

An adjacent door opened, and a man graying at the temples stepped in, wiping his hands.

"Hi, Moe," said Sandra.

"Sandra, what brings you here this morning?"

"This is Luke Martin. His car refused to start last night at the-"

Moe turned to Luke. He stared at him for a second longer. "What happened?"

Luke raised both eyebrows. "Hello…ummm…last night I was driving-and the engine sputtered and died."

Moe nodded once. "Make, model, year?"

Luke told him.

Moe opened his right palm. "Key, please."

Luke reached into his pocket and pulled out everything

plus the lining as if a policeman had asked him to empty them. He placed the key in Moe's palm.

"Okay, I'll check it out and bring it back to the workshop. It's at the restaurant, right?"

Luke nodded.

"What's the number where I can reach you?"

Luke gave him his cell number and told him he was staying at Sam Stone's house.

"Deputy Stone?" asked Moe.

"Yes," said Luke.

Okay, have a good morning. I have to get back to work. Thanks, Sandra." He gave an upward nod to Luke.

"Okay, one thing is taken care of," said Sandra as they were back in her car. "I can drop you off wherever you want to paint, just tell me when to pick you up."

"Oh Sandra, I'm so grateful for your help."

"I'm happy to do it." She wanted to add, *After all, you gave me an orgasm last night*. But she kept her mouth shut. She was already establishing boundaries. Saying something like that would only confuse him.

Minutes later, Luke directed Sandra off the road, and they took a dirt road to a clearing in the woods.

"Do you remember this place?" asked Luke after she stopped.

"Of course. I told my parents I was having a sleepover at Laura's house, and we camped out here." Sandra stopped there. Again, she didn't want to encourage him. That was just after she'd given up her V card. The first time wasn't so great, but subsequent times were mind-blowing.

Luke smiled. "The make-out spot for teenagers."

"All right, Luke, I'll come and get you later. Here." She pushed her phone toward him. "Type in your number."

Luke did and called it. Soon his phone vibrated in his

pocket. "Now I have your number too." He got out of the car and brought out his easel. He placed his stuff on the ground.

Sandra made a three-point turn and left. In the rearview mirror, she saw Luke waving and felt a tug in her heart. She still felt for him and wished things had worked out.

Back in Beaver Run, a few people were already in for breakfast. Some regulars like loggers and truck drivers. It was funny she and Megan could compete on breakfast items, but she remained open for lunch and dinner, plus the bar. But yet, they both were in the black. It was a healthy competition.

"Hi, Sandra," said one of her waiters. "Laura's mother was here earlier looking for you. Said you should call her."

"Thanks." Sandra headed for her office and called Sally as she walked.

"Hi, Sandra."

"Good morning, Sally. Mom said you told her about Luke."

Sally muttered a curse in her deep husky voice.

They spoke for about half a minute, then agreed to meet for lunch at the library.

The rest of the morning was a blur. Sandra operated on autopilot in the back office, paying bills and checking inventory, but all the time, Luke was running around in her head. Finally, noon arrived, and it was time to meet Sally.

Sandra brought two chicken salads from the restaurant in takeout containers. She knew Sally would want to give her money for it, but she would say no.

For some strange reason, Sandra got along better with Laura's mom than with her own. They had this honor code between them. Sandra could tell her things, and they would never be repeated and vice versa.

And since she was older, Sally gave her constructive advice from her own experiences.

They sat together on a bench outside the library, enjoying their lunch. Across the lawn was the police station.

"We'll be having an exhibition soon at the library," said Sally. "Sarah helped me the first time, but since that news broke, it's hard to ask her."

Sarah was Trevor's wife. She was in the news a few months ago. A damsel in distress story with a happy ending.

"Since I found out her net worth, I don't feel comfortable asking her to work."

Sandra speared some lettuce and chicken with her fork. "She's down to earth, and she volunteered. I could ask her if she was offended." She put the food in her mouth and started to chew.

"Please don't. It's not a lot of work, though. I'll ask her myself. So what is this I'm hearing? You spent the night with your ex?"

"No, I dropped him off at Stone's place. That's where he's staying. I don't know. He seems to want to start something again after-"

"After he dumped you!"

Sandra sat up and looked around to make sure nobody heard or was lurking around. Nobody was close to them. Across at the sheriff's office, she saw Stone getting into a squad car. She played with her food. "Well, yes. Last night…we…"

"I know you're not dumb enough to sleep with him. So he must have gotten you off with his clever fingers."

Sandra's nostrils flared. "Sally! Well, something like that." It'd been a long time she had sex.

"And you're thinking, *Why not?* What about Peter?" Sally snapped her fingers. "What's his last name again? Penise! I would have changed my name a long time ago no matter how much they tried to push a French pronunciation spin on it."

Sally looked down at her food, picked up a grape-sized tomato and put it in her mouth.

"Peter doesn't excite me," said Sandra. "He's more like a stable guy. He wants to start a family, and I feel I'm at that stage now. If Luke hadn't breezed into town, I would have focused on him. But that would be deceitful. Marrying for expediency, not love."

Sally swallowed. "Everybody's different. The kings and queens of old taught us that. They married for alliances and convenience. If they were lucky, love might grow on them with time. Don't forget your friend Laura. She married for love. She's the one with the baby now." Sally made air quotes in the air. "The husband is nowhere to be seen."

Sandra nodded, and her mind drifted to Luke. Maybe Sally was right. "Sorry, what did you say?"

"Girl, you have to pay attention. This is what you're going to do." Sally repeated herself.

Sandra was sure her eyes were as large as ping pong balls as Sally spoke. Face flushed with heat, she leaned closer, not sure she'd heard right. There was no way she heard right. "You want me to do what?" she whispered.

9

Luke

LUKE HADN'T ANTICIPATED WHAT HE WAS GOING THROUGH. Well, he didn't know he would meet Sandra in Beaver Run and actually get close to her again. There was a longing in his heart for Sandra. He wanted her.

Was it love or just lust? Or the challenge of not being able to have her again? What he gave up of his own free will?

Luke prepped the canvas and began painting in what would become the greenery of the forest. He had done this so many times before. His hand flew back and forth from the canvas to the color palette on autopilot as if he had eyes on his fingers.

The sound of birds calling out to each other, the occasional sound of cars passing by on the main road, and the rustle of leaves were his only companions.

. . .

It seemed like everything about him was coming to a head right here in Beaver Run. Luke was almost broke. A lot was riding on him finishing this painting, which seemed to be on course. It was the most he would make for any group batch of his artwork. He barely had enough money to pay the model for the second painting.

Oh God, the model!

Luke had forgotten about the model. He placed the brush on the pallet and took out his phone. He tapped the email icon and scrolled through his inbox-nothing. He went to the spam box—still nothing from the model. He slipped the phone into his back pocket.

He wondered if he would find an affordable model here if it came to that. Paying them would be an issue considering the car. If only the car had made it to his place. It would be much easier to pretend he wanted to get around by walking.

A gentle breeze caressed his skin, bringing with it the earthy smell of the lake. He continued to paint while his mind drifted to that night he'd spent with Sandra in this very forest. He looked around and marveled at the guts they'd had then, sleeping in the open without any form of protection. It was a risk. He shook his head and muttered, "Youthful exuberance."

He thought of his father, and a lump formed in his throat. He had wanted very much to be loved by his father. His father must have seen him as some kind of pet he was forced to look after. He'd provided the basics-food, shelter, and clothing-and that was it.

What about love? Reading bedtime stories to him? Coming to his games? His father had done none of that. Luke promised himself that if ever he had the opportunity to be a father, he would be the best dad ever.

Luke's mind drifted back to Sandra. He wished he were with her at her restaurant, or she was here with him. He chuckled and shook his head. He still couldn't picture Sandra owning a bar.

He retrieved his phone from his pocket and looked at the screen. Nothing new, and the battery bar was shrinking.

Usually, Luke would have listened to a book or played music while he painted, but without his car and a means to charge his phone, he didn't want to take the chance of his cellphone running out of juice.

It'd been about six hours since Sandra had dropped him off. Luke looked at his phone, expecting to hear the sound of an incoming text from Moe. He was naked without his car close by. He could retreat in there for a snack. Get away from the heat or take a quick nap.

Suddenly, the sky darkened. Fast-moving rain clouds gathered, hiding the sun every now and then. Luke hadn't even bothered to check the weather before coming out. Well, he always had the Cherokee around to hide from the elements.

Leaves rustled violently. Maybe the wind would blow the rain clouds further away.

Now he took refuge under a canopy formed by the branches of tall trees. The intensity of the wind looked like something that would come with lightning and thunder. It was better to be indoors if you had a chance.

Luke picked up his phone, swiped the screen with his thumb, then hesitated. He didn't want to call Sandra and destabilize her day. He put the phone back in his pocket and looked around for any form of shelter. The canvas would eventually dry if it got wet.

A drop of rain fell on his forehead. Lightning streaked across the dark afternoon sky. He pulled out his phone again. There wouldn't be any Luke left if a lightning strike found him. Then he heard the sound of a car. He looked up to see Sandra's F-150 making its way toward the clearing.

Luke smiled. He gathered the easel, canvas, and sketch pad and ran toward the car.

Sandra rolled down the window and grinned at him. "I thought I was late. It's already raining at the restaurant."

"You're right on time." He opened the back door, placed what he was carrying on the back seat, and returned to bring the paints and pallet. He put them in just as the first barrage of raindrops touched down. He shut the back door and scrambled to the front.

Luke leaned forward and kissed her on the forehead. "You just saved me. I didn't even check the forecast before coming out. Thank you."

She glanced at him, then looked away as if she were shy. "No problem."

"Oh, did the mechanic come? I've been waiting for his call. I feel so bad dragging you out of your work. You've already done so much for me."

"It's okay, I'm not complaining. It's summer, and we have a few college kids picking up the slack. I'm sorry, your car was still there when I left. I can't really say if he came and then needed to get something more to get it going."

Sandra glanced at him and looked away as if she were embarrassed by what she saw.

Luke looked himself over, glancing down at his fly in case he'd forgotten to zip up. He had peed in the bushes at one point. "Everything okay?"

"Yeah." Sandra reached behind the backseat and came up with a brown lunch bag. "Here, I thought you might be hungry."

Luke took the bag and ripped into it. It was a wrap of some sort. Then he smelled it, and his head shot up. "Roast beef, onions, jalapenos, sweet peppers, kale, and American cheese?"

Sandra smiled and nodded.

"Woman, you have the key to my heart." Unwrapping the sandwich, he took a bite, closed his eyes, and started to chew. "Oh, my God. This feels so good." He let out another moan.

"My goodness, it's only a wrap," said Sandra. "You should listen to yourself. You sound like you're making love to it."

"You have no idea. You made this to perfection."

Sandra was now back on the road, and they were headed back to town. "I'll drive by the restaurant to see if your car's still there. Did you get any work done?"

Luke had just taken a big bite, and all he could do was nod. The sound of the rain on the roof, the swish, swish, swish of the wiper from side to side were sleep-inducing.

Sandra reached behind again but came up short.

Still chewing, Luke pointed two fingers toward his eyes, pointed at Sandra, then at the road. The universal sign for *Keep your eyes on the road*. He raised himself to look at the back seat and saw a bottle of iced tea. He grabbed it and showed Sandra.

"Yeah, it's for you."

Luke swallowed. "Sandra, you're spoiling me." He shook the bottle, unscrewed it, and took a long drink. He lowered it and replaced the top. "I didn't know I was this hungry. Sandra, you just saved a life."

"You're too dramatic. Maybe you should be starved more often. It seems to make you more appreciative."

Luke let the remark pass. Just like the rain started, the intensity slowed down, then stopped. They were now on Main Street. He could see into the parking lot of Sandra's restaurant, and his car was still there.

"It seems like Moe hasn't gotten to it yet. Don't worry, you can count on me to take you around."

Should they look for another mechanic? But he knew this was a small town. Moe must have taken over the garage after Luke left Beaver Run, but he didn't want to be in anyone's bad books, so he deferred to Sandra. "What should I do?"

"Ummm…" She considered. "I know Moe, and he never disappoints. My guess is something must have come up. Why don't we give him until tomorrow? And remember, I'm still available to help. I can be your ride."

Maybe it was the way she said ride. Luke felt a stirring in his pants. Seconds later, he was rock hard.

"Do you want to hang out at the restaurant or go back to your place?"

"If you don't mind, back to my place would be fine."

"You mind if I roll down the window? I love the smell of the air and the coolness after it rains."

"Not at all. I love it too."

There was an almost silent hum as the windows came down, followed by the sound of air rushing in, filling the car with a cool after-rain smell.

Luke shut his eyes and inhaled deeply. "Nothing beats that smell."

"That's right."

Soon Sandra turned into the driveway and killed the engine. She got out of the car and picked up the container containing the paint tubes and the pallet. "I'll let you get the rest."

Luke grabbed the remainder and walked to the door. He placed the canvas down and opened the door. "After you." He walked in behind her and shut the door.

Sandra put down the art paraphernalia and headed to a window. "I'm going to let some of the stuffy air out."

"Please do. I feel like staying outside." His eyes were glued on her as she opened the blinds, unlocked the window, and raised it. Sunlight coming in from outside outlined the contours of her body.

Wait a minute. Sandra had worn jeans and a blouse when she came by this morning, but now she had on a sundress. Had she gone home to change? Maybe something important happened at work, or she'd had to meet someone. But who?

Sandra turned around. "That's better." Their eyes locked. She looked away, smoothing her dress.

Luke's eyes followed her hands, taking in her curves. *God, she's beautiful.*

"Do you have anything to drink?" asked Sandra. She was already walking toward the kitchen and the fridge. She pulled the door open and looked in, humming. "I'm thirsty. Hmmm...yes. That will do."

Luke raised an eyebrow when she turned, and two bottles of Mike's Hard Lemonade were expertly hanging by the neck between her fingers—a trick she'd learned from owning a restaurant.

Luke rummaged through the drawers, found an opener, and placed it on the island.

Sandra popped the two bottles open and pushed one toward him. "Cheers." She took a long drink.

What the fuck is going on? thought Luke. "You must be really thirsty."

"Yes, and that was the only lemonade you have. Nothing beats cold lemonade to quench your thirst. Try it."

"Remember you just gave me a sumptuous meal in the car? I'll drink later."

She put the bottle down on the table. "So you got a lot done today?"

"I had a good start. I'm more worried about the next

painting." Luke brought out his phone and went to the website where he booked models. He barely had enough money to hire one, but he wasn't going to tell Sandra that.

"Why?"

He put the zip code and hit search. It returned nothing. Luke frowned.

"Everything okay?" asked Sandra.

Luke raised a hand without taking his eyes off the phone. Heart pounding, he expanded the distance to cover, going as far as New York City. Then he got a hit. Luke realized he now had two problems—or rather one, since money could solve both. "Shit."

"What is it?"

Luke raised his head. "So sorry." He exhaled. "I'll need a model for the next drawing. The one I booked seems to have bailed on me. I can't reach her."

Sandra shrugged. "So find another one."

Luke exhaled. "The closest model I found is in New York City, and she's way out of my budget." He hadn't meant to say that.

Sandra took another pull. "For how long do you need the model? Maybe you can find someone locally."

Luke let out a nervous laugh. "I don't even want to go asking for that. It's going to be a nude with the forest in the background."

"A nude? Oh boy. I see what you mean." Sandra raised the bottle to her lips, then stopped. Her eyes narrowed. "Was that why you asked about my sister Alexis?"

10

Sandra

"Of course not," said Luke. "It's only because you asked me about my day that I thought I should see if it could get better." Luke looked at her thoughtfully. "But do you think any local girl would pose for me?"

Sandra raised an eyebrow and rested her elbow on the kitchen island. "Nude? Jesus, Luke. Unless you have a death wish. A boyfriend, brother, father…hmmm, or even a mother could poke you full of shotgun holes." Even as that came out of her lips, she felt a pang of jealousy. Sandra didn't want any other woman posing naked for him. One thing always led to another.

Luke took a deep breath and exhaled loudly through his mouth. He walked over to the fridge, opened the door, and stared inside.

Heat rushed to Sandra's neck as she remembered her discussion with Sally. It was a riot.

"Fuck him senseless," Sally had said. "He's here for only what...two weeks. He wants you. Sow your wild oats."

"Do women sow wild oats?" Sandra had asked.

"Who cares? Luke's going to leave once his work is done. You know he will. Once bitten, twice shy, right?"

Sandra had nodded. "Right."

"Nope, nope, nope," said Sally, shaking her head. "None of that nonsense! What's good for the gander is good for the goose. Once bitten..."

"Twice shy?" asked Sandra.

"No! Next time you fuck him up."

"Jesus...How?"

"I'll tell you in a second. After you're done, then...you can settle with Peter, Mr. Good Enough. Or continue to wait for the lovely Mr. Right, with millions of other women. Yours truly included."

Luke's voice brought her back to the present.

"Sandra?" Luke's fingers went *snap, snap, snap*.

"Yes?"

"You zoned out," said Luke.

"Sorry, I was thinking of your predicament."

"Oh, that's good. Any bright ideas?"

Sandra knew this was the time to execute. She watched him. The bulge of his biceps was hardly contained by the sleeve of his T-shirt. How she would love those strong arms to wrap around her. And his lips whisper sweet nothings into her ears. "Give me a few more minutes."

Heat spread through her. She was beginning to feel the effect of the alcohol. If she was going to pull this off, she needed more courage. She drank the rest of her bottle.

Luke walked over to the fridge and opened it. "This guy Stone must have excellent taste. Everything here looks expensive."

"It must be included in the cost of the rental. I'm sure he wants the best for his customers so they'll come back."

Sandra's thoughts drifted back to her meeting with Sally earlier in the day. After talking with Sally, Sandra had gone home, taken a shower, and changed her outfit.

The best way to a man's heart is through his stomach. Sandra's plan was to surprise Luke with his favorite lunch. She had done that. Now for the second-best way to a man's heart.

The vodka was doing wonders to her. A fuzzy feeling started from her stomach and had now settled between her legs. Now or never.

Luke closed the fridge and turned around. "Wow, you really must like that drink."

Sandra raised a finger and wagged it in the air as if striking an invincible nail. "You talked me into posing nude for you when I was eighteen, remember?"

Luke looked away and scratched his jaw, guilt written all over him. "Well...you asked me to draw you."

"With my clothes on!" said Sandra, enunciating each word. "But I remember"—she raised her head and stared into the distance—"you made a few sketches, then told me it would look better without my shirt."

Luke covered his eyes. "Oh God."

"Then my bra came off." She shuddered as the memories of that night long ago felt like it was happening just now. "Then you literally removed my panties with your teeth." Her legs were now shaking. He'd introduced her to oral sex, eating her pussy as if it were some kind of snack that was only available for a limited time. Gosh, she wanted his head back there so badly. But she kept her cool.

Luke was now nodding.

"You remember, right?"

"Your panties were so wet. I thought you peed."

"I was wet for you. Then you tumbled me."

Luke shook his head. "No, that's not how it happened. It was you that seduced me."

Sandra caught sight of the canvas bag on the floor in the living room. "Is the sketch there? I never got to see it."

Luke sighed. "No, I left it in my room. I'm sure it's in storage where our personal effects were kept before the house was sold."

Sandra reached for the second bottle and took a sip. "Any plans of retrieving it?"

"Maybe. Before I...before I'm done with the paintings."

Sandra drew in a breath. Sally was right after all. He was going to say *before I leave*. She exhaled, put the bottle down on the island, and walked over to him. "Since I've posed for you once"—she shrugged—"I guess I could do it again."

Luke's face lit up. "Are you sure? Or is it"—he gestured at her bottle—"Mike talking?"

"Nope, it's me talking. Just to save you the embarrassment and bad vibe you'll generate around here by asking people to pose nude for you."

Luke placed a hand on Sandra's shoulders. His eyes twinkled. "Sandra, you don't know what that would mean to me. Whatever your fee is, I would pay. Even if I have to complete the payment later on. Name your price."

Sandra chuckled. "You don't have to pay me. I'll do it in return for a favor." The thought of what she wanted out of it sent heat coursing between her legs.

"Okay," said Luke hesitantly. "What do you want me to do for you?"

"It's nothing you can't handle."

Luke thought for a second. "Okay, as long as it's nothing that would land me in jail. A fine here and a fine there I could handle. But, jail time, no." He shook his head vigorously. "I don't want to be someone's girlfriend in prison."

Sandra laughed. "Now we're getting warmer. Listen, Luke, I thought I'd gotten over you. I was doing well until you showed up. Since last night, I've never wanted anyone as much as I've wanted you."

His mouth dropped open. "But last night you didn't want me."

"I'm going to pose for you, and in return, all I want is a good fuck from you…on demand. When I want it, and when you want it. I need to get you out of my system…whatever it takes."

Luke looked at the empty bottle on the table and then the second one. He cocked his head to the left, then to the right.

"Are you messing with me? Is it the alcohol talking?"

"No," said Sandra, shaking her head. She bit her lower lip and batted her eyelids. "Last night, you wanted to fuck me, right?" Her voice was smokey-sexy.

Luke swallowed. "Yes." His voice was hoarse and tight. "So much that I jerked off after you left."

Excitement rushed through her body like she was getting overcooked. "Well—" She raised her sundress to reveal black lacy panties.

"My God," whispered Luke.

"You can fuck me right now if you want to. And…for the next two weeks until you are done with your painting and leave town."

11

Luke

LUKE'S COCK WENT FROM ZERO TO STEEL IN THREE SECONDS. He was sure this was a prank. The lub dub, lub dub of his heartbeat sounded like three people's hearts beating all at once.

He looked around, expecting someone to jump out and say, "Boo! Now smile, you're on Prank Camera."

Luke wanted so much to run his palms over the smoothness of her skin and cup her ass. "Can you…say that again?"

"What do you want?" asked Sandra.

"Hold on. I just want to make sure we're on the same page here. You will pose for me naked until I'm done with my painting." Luke pointed at her, then at himself. "In return, you and I will have to fuck."

Sandra nodded. "I…I need to get you out of my system and move on. You can fuck me any which way you want."

Happiness bubbled in his stomach and blurted out of his lips as an uncontrolled laugher. This was the stuff of fantasy.

The type of wishes teenage boys made when they blew out the candles on their birthday cakes. And grown men make when they receive their first big bonus check.

Luke was giddy with excitement. His Mr. Happy was ecstatic. There was no more room in his pants. He might as well bring him out to get some fresh air.

"You don't believe me?" Sandra took off her sandals and hitched her dress up. She slipped her thumbs into the band of her panties and slowly slid them down. They got stuck at her hips. She wriggled...and they cleared her hips.

Luke exhaled, mesmerized.

Sandra's underwear came down her thighs and legs and settled on her ankles. She kicked them off her feet, bent down, and picked them up. "Here." She handed them over to him.

Luke felt like he was in a dream. Her panties were wet, just like old times. He put them into the back pocket of his jeans, reached under her dress, and cupped her ass.

Sandra sucked in air.

Luke growled. "I love how you feel in my hands."

They were breathing each other's air. He came closer, their lips touching.

"I love the way you grab my ass," said Sandra, breathless. "Squeeze it."

Luke did.

Her hot breath, with a hint of vodka and lemonade, hit his face. She moaned. "That feels good."

Luke kissed her. Her mouth was hot... and it tasted sweet and bitter. He delved in deeper and deeper. Their tongues did the snake dance.

"Luke." She pulled at his T-shirt as if trying to pull it straight off his body.

He reached for the hem of her dress. Sandra raised her

hands, and he pulled it over her head. He ran his palms up and down her arms.

She shuddered, her skin covered with goose pimples.

Luke took a step back, feasting his eyes on her nakedness. She really meant what she said. Expecting her to change her mind anytime, he knew he had to act fast.

Luke extended his hands. "Come with me." He walked her over to the couch. "What's your fantasy?"

Sandra batted her eyelashes. "I…I-"

"Sit. I know what you want."

Sandra let out a trembling breath. "Oh God." She flopped down.

Luke was on his knees. He wrapped his palms around her hips and slid her to the edge of the couch.

Sandra gasped.

Luke spread her thighs wide and hitched her dress up, exposing the dark glistening landing strip between her legs. It beckoned to him to wrap his lips over it, licking and sucking for all he was worth, but he'd get to that later. First things first. He ran his hands from her left thigh down to her toes. He lifted her left foot, massaging and kneading.

"Oh, that feels good. Please don't stop."

"I wouldn't stop even if a gun was pointed at me," said Luke. "Just lie back and relax."

Sandra let out a sigh and flopped back on the couch.

Luke felt her hands on his hair, caressing his scalp as if he were some kitty cat.

His lips began the climb to the promised land. Planting kisses on her calf, he squeezed and kneaded as he worked his way up.

"You really know what I need, Luke," she moaned and ran the tips of her fingers along his ears, lips, and all over his face.

Luke placed his lips on her legs, rubbing his lips up and down, her moans exciting him the more. His cock screamed to be let out, but he ignored it. His duty was to deliver for Sandra. He continued north and arrived at her muscular thighs shaped by years of running. He ran wet circles with his tongue, then sucked her mid-thigh.

Sandra moaned. "Oh Luke." Laughter burst out of her as her whole body shuddered, her thighs clamped around his head. "It tickles. More!"

Luke loved Sandra's sexy voice. Her *You're doing a great job* voice always excited him. He did the same to her right thigh, wetting circles around the soft skin of her inner thigh. Sucking deep down, he felt her whole body tremble. He felt the pressure of her hands encouraging him to continue north. But that was the main course, and Luke was in no hurry.

He rested his chin on her landing strip and shifted his chin to the right, then to the left, rubbing her clit. Her breath hitched each time he moved his head, and he savored the experience.

"Luke."

He reached under her bra and covered her breasts with his hands.

A deep-seated moan escaped her lips and intensified when he squeezed.

Luke groaned. "You feel so great in my hands." His fingers found her nipples and rolled them until they were rock hard.

"Yes, Luke, yes. So good, more."

Luke grinned at her instruction. He pulled her nipples.

Sandra gasp-moaned as he squeezed harder.

Luke rubbed his lips against her stomach, then began a wet trail down. Her stomach muscles quivered with anticipation.

. . .

"Luke, eat it." She pushed his head, trying to direct his mouth to where she wanted it to be.

Luke resisted. Not because he was cocky, but for her own good. He wanted to bring her close to the edge and then pull back, hopefully intensifying the sensation for her. His erection was like a water pipe. He needed to bury it inside her.

"Down, Luke…"

He obliged her. He licked his way down, past her clit to her pussy lips. He knew all her buttons, but it'd been a long time. He wanted to make sure those triggers were still the same.

His eyes fixed on hers as he nibbled, pulled, and tugged at her pussy lips. He dipped his tongue into her core. The unique Sandra Leigh nectar coated his tongue. He recorded and filed away every move, sound, and expression she made as he licked, sucked, tugged, and pulled.

Sandra pressed her thighs around his head, whimpering. "Luke…yes. Oh gosh, yes, I missed this."

Her feet, crisscrossed behind his shoulders, rubbed his back as she writhed and moaned. "Luke…I need to…"

Luke pulled back from her pussy. "You need what?" He knew what she wanted. But he wanted her to say it. He caught her pussy lips with his and nibbled. Her fingers dug deeper into his scalp.

Her reaction was getting him hot and bothered. If he wasn't careful, he would cream his boxers without even unleashing his cock. "Fuck! What do you need, Sandra?"

"I want to come! Please make me come!" she breathed.

Those words were magic to his ears. Luke pulled back from her pussy. He reached for his jeans, released the buckle, unbuttoned it, and released his cock.

Sandra definitely sensed the change in the equation. She untangled her legs from his shoulders, turned around, kneeled, and crouched low. "Now Luke. Please, now."

A deep groan escaped his throat.

Her pussy lips glistened, calling to him.

Luke sprang to his feet, took off his T-shirt, and tossed it. Pulling his boxers and jeans down, he took off his shoes and kicked his pants off. He looked at her butt, heart-shaped and juicy. Luke couldn't resist. He slapped her butt cheeks.

Sandra gasped.

Luke grabbed her waist as if trying to encircle it and pulled her toward him. His cock nudged against her cheeks. "Sandra, I've been dreaming about this moment for a long time." His voice was tight and deep. "I'm going to slip my cock into your sweet wet pussy. Fill you up." The tip of his cock found her core, and he pushed in slowly. Her wet heat engulfed him.

Sandra moaned.

"Gosh, you're so tight, so tight," said Luke. He was tempted to go fast, but he also wanted to take her to the brink and back again without losing control himself.

Sandra gasped as his clock slipped in. "That feels so good." She thrust back, and soon his long, thick cock was buried to the hilt.

Luke pulled back, her pussy held tight, adding more friction. He shuddered, the sensation out of this world. He plunged back in slowly, enjoying the pleasures she offered. Again, she thrust into him. He pulled back. He had to focus on something else. He reached for her breast, found her nipples, and rolled them in his fingers.

Sandra moaned. "Yes." She slammed back into him.

"Give it to me," said Luke through tight lips. Change of plans. He didn't think he could hold it any longer. He opted to speed things up. He slid his hand back to her pussy. As he thrust into her, his finger worked back and forth over her clit.

"Yes…that's the spot. Faster, deeper."

Luke worked her clit as fast as he could while Sandra thrust back, slamming into him again and again.

He wanted to get her off first. The sound of sex filled the room. Skin against skin. Wet pussy penetrated by a hard cock.

"Don't stop. You're slaying me. Don't stop. More! I'm almost there."

Luke leaned forward and grunted in her ear. "You've finished me. You feel so good inside." He couldn't believe how he'd lived all these years without this pussy.

Sandra arched her back, her breath coming in gasps. She slammed into Luke over and over again.

Luke finally abandoned the grip he had on his control. He grabbed her butt, pushing and pulling. He felt like he was in a relay race and had just been handed the baton for the last dash.

Sandra gave as good as she got, pushing back. "My goodness," she said, breathless. "I never knew doggy style could be so much fun."

Sweat trickled down Luke's neck onto his chest. He straddled the sharp edge of orgasm, holding on, not wanting to tip over to the other side. He reached under her and stroked her clit faster.

Sandra let out a deep moan.

Luke felt her pussy tighten around his cock as she started to come. He grabbed her hips and pulled her toward him, burying his cock deeper inside her. Luke groaned as his release tore through him, flooding her pussy.

Luke's legs trembled, barely able to hold him. He held her tight as he collapsed on top of her, not letting go.

12

Sandra

SANDRA WOKE WITH A START. DID HER ALARM GO OFF? SHE sat up and looked around, confirming what she already knew: Luke had left. She stretched her hand to the bedside table and retrieved her phone. The alarm hadn't gone off yet.

Sandra contemplated whether she should go for a run or not. Isn't mind-blowing sex considered exercise? She took a deep breath-she could still smell him around her.

Sandra smiled. Her head, pussy, nipples-her whole body ached in a sweet way. Since college, she'd never drunk that much alcohol so fast. But she'd needed courage to make her demands on Luke, and it had worked. But it was worth it.

Her mind drifted to a few hours ago at his place. They'd dozed off on the sofa, spent. When they awoke, she'd wanted to go home.

"No problem," said Luke. "I'll drop you."

At first, she was puzzled, then realized where he was

coming from. Sandra felt fine. Most of the alcohol was out of her system, she believed. She hadn't even been tipsy to begin with, only tired. "No, I can drive."

"So can I, and I had zero to drink. Unless you count the ones I got from kissing your lips. Don't worry, I'll drop you off and jog back."

They got back to Sandra's place, and she went to take a shower. She'd just gotten the water temperature right in the shower when the door opened, and Luke had joined her.

Sandra got a good look at him. He'd definitely added more muscles since they were in school. His chest was well-contoured, his six-pack prominent. He was naked and sporting a massive erection.

Luke moved behind her. "Can I have the sponge, please?"

Sandra felt his cock stab her backside. She handed him the sponge, her body shaking with anticipation.

Luke scrubbed her back, then ran the soapy sponge from her neck down to her armpits, one after the other. Then her breasts. He scrubbed gently in a circular motion, caressing her nipples, down her stomach.

Sandra whimpered, drawing her head back, so the water jet hit between her breasts. "God, you're good." She spread her legs as he scrubbed her pubs, then her crotch. Her leg shook.

"You like that?" asked Luke as he nuzzled her neck and continued washing with the sponge.

Sandra brushed her butt against his cock and heard his sharp intake of air. It was just like old times. Apart from when they'd just started dating years ago, sex in the bathroom was a no-no. Too risky. Slipping and falling wasn't sexy. They instead turned it into a no-penetration, tactile, sensual experience.

Luke paused to add more soap to the sponge.

Sandra moaned and threw her head back, the water heating her face and cascading down her body. She was on fire. She wanted more, but right now, she settled with anticipation.

Then it was her turn to wash him. She was behind him and spent some time on his cock, running both hands back and forth along his shaft, enjoying his moans as she brought him to the edge and then backed away.

Luke stayed back after she got out of the shower, hoping to deflate his erection with a cold shower.

"If it doesn't work, come to the bed. I have another idea."

Luke laughed. "Now it's even gotten harder." He turned the shower off. "It's no use. You should have kept your mouth shut."

Sandra looked at him and batted her eyelashes. "Are you sure about that?"

"About what?"

She ran the tip of her tongue along her lips. "About keeping my mouth shut."

Luke's cock jerked.

As she dried her hair, Sandra watched him standing there like one of those Greek statues in museums, but with a hard-on.

She bit her lower lip and tossed him a towel. Luke preferred to dry himself while inside the shower, so when he came out, he dried his feet on the mat and was done. He hated wet floors.

He dried himself, then brought his arm to his nose and sniffed. "Now I smell like a woman. I hope I don't attract the wrong crowd."

Luke wrapped the towel around his waist. His towel now looked like a camping tent.

Sandra smiled. "Don't worry, you've already attracted the

right crowd." Standing by the door and wrapped in a towel already, she motioned with a finger for him to come.

"You're really enjoying this, aren't you?"

"It's a win-win for both of us. You get your model, and I get you out of my system."

Luke nodded.

"Moreover, you're not jogging or running anywhere just after taking a shower."

Luke shrugged. "Well, that makes sense."

She led the way to her bed. Since she'd returned to Beaver Run and moved into the house, she'd never invited any man over.

Sandra felt so good. If she and Luke were a married couple, would they still role-play and have this much fun?

All the shyness she felt before was gone. She unwrapped her towel.

Luke inhaled sharply. He groaned as he exhaled, his eyes feasting on her body.

"Now lose the towel."

"You're beautiful. I can't wait to put you on a canvas."

Sandra folded her towel and dropped it on the floor. She stepped closer to Luke, and touched his nipples, rolling them between her fingers. She got on her tippy toes and kissed him. His cock poked her stomach, sharing its warmth with her.

He took her mouth, nibbling and pulling at her lips, his tongue darting in and out of her mouth.

Sandra pinched his nipples, and a low moan rumbled deep inside him. She pulled back from his lips and began a slow descent, raking her nails along his body as she went down.

His cock jumped as if an electric current had touched it. "Sandra, that feels so good."

Sandra played cat and mouse with his jumpy cock. She

didn't want to use her hands to capture it. She opened her mouth wide and wrapped her lips over the head.

Luke groaned. "Yes, baby."

She looked up at him and released his cock. "This won't be like before. When you come this time, I'll swallow...all of it."

A trembling breath rushed out of Luke as he nodded. "Fuck, Sandra."

His eyes urged her to keep going, pleading with her to take him in her mouth again.

She held his cock by the base and planted small butterfly kisses along his shaft, then ran circles with her tongue over the mushroom helmet of his cock.

Sandra cupped and hefted his balls. She rolled them in her palm. The change in his breathing spoke volumes.

His hands went into her scalp and massaged it.

Sandra moaned. She loved it when her hair was messed with.

She ran her tongue underneath his shaft from the base to the tip, leaving a wet trail on his shaft.

Luke rewarded her with a teardrop precum at the tip.

Sandra's tongue shot out and lapped it up. She looked at his cock and still couldn't believe that after all these years, it was hers again to fuck and suck as she pleased.

Luke groaned as Sandra swallowed him inch by inch. She held the base of his shaft and bobbed her head back and forth.

Luke slid his hands into her hair, and when he spoke, his voice quavered. "This is beautiful...you are beautiful." He massaged her scalp, and soon his hands were directing her head.

Sandra's free fingers found her pussy, and she rubbed her clit as she sucked him. Doing both simultaneously reminded her of when she learned how to drive. Initially, she couldn't drive and listen to music at the same time. But here she was, sucking a cock and rubbing herself in synchrony.

Luke thrust his hips forward, helping her work him. "That's it, Sandra. Your mouth is the best ever." He seemed to notice what her hand was doing. "Hmmm, your fingers...my goodness. Can I taste?"

Sandra didn't hesitate. She plunged another finger into her wetness then raised it up to him.

Luke grabbed her hand like his life depended on it. He licked them, then took them in his mouth, mimicking what she was doing to his cock. "Sandra." His voice was raspy and low. "Sweetheart, I can't..."

Did he just call her sweetheart? What men say and do when you have their cock in your mouth. The power she had at that moment excited her. Luke let go of her hand and held her hair with both hands. Excited, her hands shot back to her pussy.

Luke ran his hands over her hair as his cock went in and out of her mouth. He was literally fucking her mouth. His legs started to shake.

Sandra's fingers moved faster over her clit. Without warning, an orgasm swept through her. "Oh God," she whimpered. Surprised by the intensity. She could always get herself off, but this was...

Luke was now grunting. Excited by her orgasm and knowing he was seconds away from coming, he tapped her shoulder.

Sandra looked up.

He opened his mouth to speak, but only gasps escaped his throat.

Sandra knew he was warning her. His cock was about to

reward her. In response, she wrapped her hands behind him and pulled him forward.

His pubic hair tickled her nose. Before she could process that, his cock got bigger inside her mouth.

Hot jets splashed against the back of her throat, activating her swallow reflex. She took it all down and held Luke as he trembled and gasped. She sucked the last drop out of him and licked him clean.

Breathing hard, Luke reached down and cupped her face in his palm. "Thank you."

Sandra got up. "You're welcome." She clapped her hands together, proud of myself.

Four years ago, she had never been able to get Luke off with just her mouth and hands, even though he'd showed her what he liked.

"Do you have anything to eat?"

She walked toward her closet. "Sure. Let me slip into something, and I'll make you whatever you want to eat."

She wasn't going to eat, but she made him sausages, sunny side up eggs, bacon, and toast for dinner. Then they went to bed after that.

The bah, bah, bah of her phone alarm pulled her out of her reverie. Her phone alarm was right on time. But where was Luke? She needed him to put out the fire between her legs.

Sandra put on a robe and went looking for him. When she walked into the kitchen, she immediately saw the yellow stick-it-note on the fridge. The message read 'Jogged to my place. Pick me up en-route to the restaurant.'

Sandra smiled. Oh well, she might as well go for her morning run. For the next forty-five minutes, she pounded the trail.

She'd just walked into her home and looking forward to getting ready and going to pick Luke up when a text came in.

It was from Luke and read 'Stone dropped by. Now I'm being hijacked. I'll text you later.'

"What the…" said Sandra out loud.

13

Luke

Luke was still processing all that had happened in the past six hours. Maybe coming to Beaver Run wasn't such a bad idea after all.

The smell of her soap all around him had him thinking about her. He thought of last night-Sandra on her knees, her big eyes looking up at him with his dick in her mouth. He started to get hard. Thank God he was wearing basketball shorts and an oversized T-shirt. Was it even possible? Getting a boner while running. Well, there it was. Luke smiled.

He wracked his brain on why Sandra would come up with such a proposal. Was she trying to trick her own mind? He chuckled as he ran. No, that's not the current word. Give herself permission to have sex with him without the guilt. Luke's smile faded.

He remembered how sad she had been the day he left. Four years ago. How she must have felt over the years, used, and discarded. Not wanted. He knew that feeling. His father was always mad, as if he'd offended him in some way. Pushing him away without laying a finger on him.

"Beep! Beep!"

Luke jumped. He had drifted into the middle of the road. He waved his regrets and continued running closer to the sidewalk.

His thoughts drifted back to Sandra. What if she was serious about getting him out of her system for good? Like gorging yourself on a particular food so you'll hate it.

He knew she still felt something for him, but she didn't want to be hurt again. What about him? Did he still care?

Luke ran faster as if he was trying to outrun his thoughts. He'd wronged her. But how could he make it right?

Settle down in Beaver Run? He doubted it, but he would give it a chance. Sandra had given him all the reason any full-blooded man needed to stick to a girl. He still had feelings for her. Even four years ago, when he left, he'd had feelings for her. But pursuing his career seemed to be the best move.

Sweat poured down his body as he ran into the driveway of the Airbnb. He did stretching exercises for his calf and thighs, then went into the house. A shower, maybe some food. No, Sandra would probably have plans for breakfast.

Feeling a lot better with himself and his plan to treat Sandra better, he jumped into the shower, humming as he scrubbed himself.

Luke got out of the shower and had just put on a fresh pair of jeans and a blue shirt sleeve shirt when the doorbell rang, immediately followed by a knock.

Luke smiled. Sandra must have seen his note. As he got closer, he noticed the silhouette on the order side of the glazed decorative glass on the door was a lot bigger than Sandra's. Who could it be?

He unlocked the door and pulled it open. He stared into

the happy smiling face of a man in a green sheriff deputies' uniform. The face was familiar.

"Hello!"

At first, Luke thought it was Trevor. No, he knew Trevor. Trevor couldn't have changed that much in such a short time. Then he realized it was the guy he'd seen in the picture on the fridge—the house owner.

"Sam Stone?"

"Yes! You must be Luke Martin." He extended his hand. "For a second, I thought you were a snob." He laughed. "Call me Stone. Everybody calls me Stone. No, Adela calls me Rock."

Luke shook his hand. "Luke."

"Sorry, I hope I didn't get you at a bad time. I was just driving by and said I might as well drop in and say hello."

"Not at all. Come in." Luke stepped to the side, and Stone entered. "No, I just got ready. I was about to text Sandra and remind her to pick me up on her way. By the way, thanks for renting to me. It's such a nice place."

"Don't mention it. I'm glad you chose me, and not some fancy hotel in Mountain Peak. Oh, I heard about your car." Stone smiled and shrugged with his palms open. "You know, Beaver Run is a small town, and you're someone that grew up here. Any luck with Moe? He's a genius with engines, but he's busy."

"No, he didn't get to it yesterday. Hopefully today, so I'll stop bothering Sandra. She's been such a godsend."

"I could give you a ride. You know we grab some coffee, give Sandra a break…"

Luke didn't want to impose on him. "I don't want to take you out of your way-"

"No problem. The least I can do for the guy renting my

place is give him a ride into town. Just send Sandra a text. I'm sure she wouldn't mind."

Luke nodded. "Thanks." He sent a text to Sandra.

"You're an artist, right?"

Luke looked up. "Yeah."

"Are you any good?"

Luke's stomach tightened. "Ummm…"

"Just kidding! You should have seen your face. There must be something in the water here. A lot of creatives here. There's Priyanka Patel. She's an artist too. Her parents live on millionaire row."

"Millionaire row?"

"That's what I call that part of town on Beech Street with huge mansions."

"Yes, I know the area," said Luke. "Vacation homes for the rich to hide away."

"My fiancée writes, then you."

"Adela Williams?"

"Yes, you know her?"

"Well, there's only one elementary school, middle school, and high school here. All the kids went there. But Sandra told me you two are together now. Adela's an author?"

"Yep. She wrote a novel about how we met." Stone looked at his watch. "Why don't we get breakfast, and I'll tell you all about it on the way. I can drop you off where you are painting."

"Okay, let me grab my stuff."

Stone looked at the unfinished canvas and let out a whistle. "That's taking shape nicely. I'm always intrigued when brushstrokes eventually come together to create something beautiful."

Luke liked Stone. But he didn't like getting into the

cruiser. There was something about police cars that made him jumpy.

Stone told him about moving to New Jersey and the incident that led to him meeting Adela. "Your life was in danger."

"I guess so, but then I didn't realize it."

They stopped at Megan's. Luke ordered the same thing he'd gotten yesterday.

Stone got a breakfast bowl with eggs, sausages, harsh, and bacon. He also ordered a dozen donuts.

"For the break room at the station," he said as they left. "Are you running late or anything?"

Luke shook his head. "No, why?"

"The station is just around the corner. I'll drop it off, then I'll drop you."

"Fine with me."

Stone drove to the station. He parked and asked Luke if he wanted to come in.

"Maybe some other time."

Stone grabbed the box of donuts from the back of the car. "I'll be right back."

Moments later, another cruiser parked beside Stone's. The driver's face was familiar. Their eyes locked. It was Trevor.

Trevor frowned, then his lips parted in a smile.

Luke smiled back and waved.

"Hey Luke!" said Trevor as soon as he got out of the car. "I heard you were back. Good to see you."

Luke opened the door and stepped out. "Good to see you too. Sheriff, huh?"

"Deputy. I heard you were back in town—from who now... someone mentioned it. Back for good?"

Luke didn't know how to answer. Jesus, he was fucking

the guy's sister. "I'm still working on some paintings. We'll see how it goes."

"Trevor!" said a hoarse female voice to their right. "It's too early to be chatting."

"Oh, oh." Trevor faked a cringy look. "It's the authority. Good morning, Clara."

Luke watched the gray-haired woman Trevor had called Clara, probably in her sixties, walk toward them. Her face looked familiar. Luke smiled at her and said, "Good morning."

The woman scowled. "There's nothing good about this morning." She looked at him. "By the way, who are you? A perp?"

Trevor chuckled. "Clara! Look at him, don't you recognize him?"

Clara squinted, then cocked her head. "I can say the only person you remind me of is the late Mrs. Martin..." She covered her mouth with her palms. "Good lord, Luke?"

Luke's eyes darted from Trevor to Clara. "Ah, yes."

"You have your father's build, but your mother's face. I used to change your diapers. Give me a hug. So good to see you." She spread out her hands.

Luke hugged her. "You knew my mother?"

Clara mimicked him. "*You knew my mother?* Of course. I used to babysit you after your...ah, memories." She shook her head. "After your mother passed. Sorry about your father. Are you back for good?"

That question again. "I have a commission to produce artwork here."

"He's an artist," said Trevor.

"Wow, just like your mother. You have to do an exhibition at the library."

Luke smiled, but said nothing. He didn't do exhibitions.

Clara pinched his cheek. "Good to see you again. Gentlemen, I have to leave. See you around, Luke." She headed toward the entrance.

"Clara practically was a babysitter at one point or the other to all the adults in this town," said Trevor.

"I heard that," said Clara.

Luke glanced at the lady as she walked away and wondered if she could tell him more about his mother.

Just then, Stone ran out of the station. "Hi, Clara. I left some donuts in the backroom."

"Haven't you heard that donuts will make your clothes shrink?" She disappeared into the building.

Luke laughed. "Is she always that funny?"

"Hilarious," said Stone as he walked toward Luke and Trevor. He turned to Trevor. "Hi."

"Hey, I see you've met Luke," said Trevor.

"Yes, I stopped over at my place to formally welcome him, then we came over to drop off donuts. Anyway, I have to go drop him so he can continue with his masterpiece."

Trevor nodded. "Where are you painting?"

"The side of the lake where teenagers hang out. Later, I'll paint by the hanging bridge."

"My dad loves to fish close to that bridge," said Trevor.

Stone looked at him. "We have to run. We should hang out one of these nights at Beaver Tail."

Trevor shook hands with Luke. "Yes, we should. It's a pleasure seeing you again. Take care."

"Pleasure's all mine." Luke got back in the car and prayed that all would end well. He hoped he wouldn't disappoint any of these friendly folks.

14

Sandra

SANDRA DROVE TOWARDS HER PARENTS' HOUSE. IF THERE were any new stories about her and Luke, her mother would know.

Sandra felt a calmness she hadn't felt in a long time. As if something she'd always worried about had now been taken off her shoulder, freeing up her mind.

Maybe because she'd hooked up with an old flame. There was familiarity.

Familiarity.

Perhaps that's what Okafor's Law was all about. She and Luke just picked up from where they stopped. She hoped in the next week or so, she would be able to get him out of her system. That should help her adjust when he eventually packed up and left.

Sandra was close to their family home when contradictory thoughts crossed her mind. What if her mother was the one asking probing questions? Her mother knew her well, and

Sandra was sure it showed that she'd been well fucked after a long drought.

She might start asking questions like, *Didn't he dump you before?* Sandra decided to drive to the restaurant instead. She would rather enjoy herself for the next few weeks without any negative talk.

Her mind drifted to the painting. Would it be like the first time she posed for him? She'd forgotten it wasn't all roses and sunshine to pose for a painting. She would have to sit in a particular pose for hours. It would be drudgery, but the thought filled her with positive thoughts. His eyes on her would feel like butterfly feathers caressing her skin.

A fussy feeling started from her stomach and settled between her legs. She wanted him again. If only he hadn't run off to get back to his place so early.

Sandra drove into the restaurant and headed to the staff parking in the back. She caught a glimpse of a white car in the parking lot. Yes, it was Luke's car all right. She was surprised it was still there. If Moe didn't show by noon, she would call him.

She parked and locked her car, then headed for the back door of the restaurant. Sandra glanced at the garbage enclosure. Good, it hadn't been tampered with. Every now and then in the summer, bears came down from the mountains to forage for food. That wouldn't be a problem since not everyone finished the food they were served. However, bears never clean up after themselves and leave a mess.

Last summer, a family in the next town over found a mama bear with her cubs cooling off in their swimming pool.

Sandra pulled the back door open and entered. The first person she saw was Cletus Marshal.

"Hello, busy morning already?"

Cletus Marshal was the chef and had stayed on after

Sandra bought into the bar. He was a sixty-something-year-old bull of a man. He had planned to retire and tour the world with his wife but decided to stay on a few more years until Sandra got things figured out.

"Good morning," said Cletus. "A large group dropped in for breakfast, and we are working on their order. A whole busload."

"Nice. That's a good problem to have, right?"

Cletus continued, "One of them asked me if they could use Beaver Tail as a rest stop. They'll be bringing tourists with them a couple days a week for sightseeing. They'll let us know beforehand when they're coming, so they won't overwhelm us."

"Hmmm, what do you think?" asked Sandra.

Cletus nodded. "That'll be excellent for business. We treat them well. Fill their bellies with good food, and they'll tell their friends about Beaver Tail." He chuckled. "Word of mouth is the best form of advertising. Once we know when they'll be here, we increase the inventory for breakfast stuff like eggs, bread, butter, for the days we know they'll be stopping by."

Sandra nodded slowly, liking the idea more.

Cletus pointed out the person to talk to. A Mr. Murphy. A big man, probably more than six feet tall with a large girth. He wore a straw hat, the visible part of his hair gray. "Do you need help anywhere?" asked Sandra when she saw the number of people.

"No, we're fine." He nodded toward the table. "Go get more business."

Sandra touched him on the shoulder. "Thank you."

"Anytime," said Cletus and headed to the kitchen.

Sandra took a deep breath, then walked over to the man. "Mr. Murphy?"

"That's me. Edward Murphy. Call me Ed. You must be the owner of this fine establishment."

"Co-owner. Please call me Sandra." They shook hands.

"Sandra, we love the food. Just give me a yes or no. If yes, we'll sort the rest out by email."

If Cletus hadn't given his blessing, Sandra would have overthought things and probably refused. "Yes."

"Great! This is my business card. My email and phone number are there. We can conclude the deal via email."

Sandra gave him her own business card, and that was it. There wasn't really much to talk about. A large group would be coming by a few days a week, and they'd give them a break on prices.

She went into her office to take care of the daily task of running the business. There was always something going on. The chef and the other guys at the bar all did an excellent job, but she would place the orders to replenish inventory. Pay utility bills, the staff salary, and any other thing that came up.

Sandra was working on the salaries when there was a knock on her door. She looked up, knowing the door would be opened right away. It was a knock and open policy.

Laura poked her head in.

Sandra smiled. "Hey." Her eyes darted to the wall clock.

"Aren't you going to eat today?"

"My God! Where did the time go?"

Laura walked into the office. "You know what they say. Time flies when you're having fun. I thought I'd eat with you and hear some gossip. I'm on my lunch break."

"I'll order something from the restaurant," said Sandra and pushed back from her seat. "We can sit outside. What should I order for you?"

Five minutes later, they sat outside watching traffic as they waited for their food.

Sandra took a sip from her drink, then checked her phone. No text from Luke. "How's Zoe?" Zoe was Laura's daughter and Sally's granddaughter.

Her friend smiled. "She's with her grandma at the library having a blast."

"Oh, that's nice."

"I'll pick her up after my shift."

"You'll probably spend the night at your mom's place then."

Laura chuckled. "That's more likely. Zoe will be sleeping by the time I get there."

They both turned to look at a waiter that arrived with their food. He smiled and raised a plate. "Tuna sandwich?"

Laura reached for it. "That's mine."

"Beef burger, well done." He placed it in front of Sandra and also two glasses of Diet Coke.

"Thank you," said Laura. "It's James, right?"

"No, I'm John," said the waiter with a smile. "James is the other twin."

"Oh gosh, I'm so sorry."

"It's all right. We get it all the time. The burden of being a twin."

"John, I'd like another burger, well done, with fries, in a to-go bag, please."

"Sure." He nodded and left.

"You're getting it for Luke?" asked Laura, then took a bite of her wrap.

"Yeah. He's out in the woods painting." She looked at her phone again. "I'll take lunch to him there since his car is still incapacitated." She glanced at the parking lot just to make sure. His car was still there. "We're waiting for Moe to take a look. I guess he's been busy." Should she call Moe? Once his car was fixed, what excuse would she have to see him then?

"How's it going with him? You didn't fill me in on how that night went." Laura smiled. "And the way you're checking your phone, it seems like your garden was plowed and some of the weeds pulled out. But it needs more work."

Sandra tried to keep a poker face. "Have you been hanging out with Stone and Adela? All this talk about farming."

Laura sighed. "Are you guys back together? "Did you…" Laura bit her lower lip, made a circle with her left thumb and forefinger, bent her right thumb, and inserted it into the circle. Thrusting in and out, breathing heavily.

Sandra feigned embarrassment. "Oh God." She looked away, not wanting to say anything.

"He looked good. I'm sure you were on your back once he asked." Laura waited to be filled in. "Okay, you don't want to talk about it."

"Nothing new yet. I dropped him off by the lake yesterday to paint, picked him up just before the rain started, and took him to his place." Sandra changed the subject. "I had lunch with your mom yesterday." She took a big bite of her burger so she wouldn't have to answer any questions without thinking.

Laura swallowed and frowned. "What do you guys even talk about? I hope she's not giving you relationship advice." She started to work on her own sandwich.

Sandra didn't want to tell her friend what her mother had said. It was between the two of them. "Nothing much. Just the local gossip. She mentioned she's planning to host an art exhibition at the library."

Laura nodded. "She mentioned that too." Laura took another bite and spoke with food in her mouth. "Sometimes, I think she tries to relieve her life from the advice she gives. So take them with a pinch of salt or at least evaluate them before you plunge in. She once told me years ago, the fastest way to get a guy out of your system was to fuck him nonstop for two weeks straight." She shook her head. "Duh. The only thing that could lead to is pregnancy."

Heat rushed to Sandra's cheeks. Luckily, Laura was scrutinizing her sandwich, trying to figure out where to take the next bite. Sandra was fine in that department. She'd never stopped taking the pill. Didn't want to break the habit and then have to relearn it again.

"How did you guys start dating in high school? I can't remember. It was like one minute Luke was the introverted kid that kept to himself and you were too shy to even look a guy in the face. The next, you two were dating and inseparable."

Sandra smiled and picked at her fries. "It was in art class. I liked art but could barely draw. One day he was finishing his assignment in class, and I happened to notice his drawing. I was amazed by his skill and stood behind him, watching. After a while, he stopped painting."

Laura shrugged. "Why?"

"He said he couldn't draw with me watching him. So I told him to pretend I wasn't there. Then he said he couldn't. He said it would have been easy if I wasn't so pretty."

"Oh, my goodness. That's the worst line ever." Laura was quiet for a moment. "But, coming from him, it wasn't a line at all. He meant it."

"Exactly. Then Luke offered to draw me. I was flattered, and I agreed. During the session, he somehow talked me out of my T-shirt, jeans, bra, and panties."

"That's a fairy tale. And you guys were together until college when he decided to wander off, and now he's back again. Men!" Laura shook her head. "You know what?"

"What?"

"I'll give you the same advice my mother gave me. Fuck his brains out for the next two weeks and get him out of your system. Just don't get pregnant. It always changes the equation."

Sandra's mouth dropped open.

15

Luke

STONE HAD DROPPED LUKE OFF AT THE SAME SPOT WHERE he'd painted yesterday.

Luke thought Stone was the kind of guy you'd want to go out for a beer with. He couldn't remember what Adela looked like, but he knew the Williams farm. He was sure if he saw Adela, he would remember. The guy must be in love to have abandoned his home, and moved in with his girl on a farm.

That was what men in love did, thought Luke. He knew that wasn't him. With time he would probably get to meet everybody again.

Trevor was friendly too. He didn't bring up Sandra, and Luke was thankful for that. Sandra was a grown woman, and her relationships should be her business unless some law was broken.

Then there was Clara. He never knew she had been his babysitter, but he sure did remember seeing her around. Like everyone else, she'd gotten older. Maybe before he left, he would sit down with her and see what he could learn about his mother.

The rain really did a good job. The woods felt cooler and smelled of grass and earth. Birds chirped high up in the trees.

He knew that within the next hour or two, things would start to heat up again. He unfolded the easel, hung the canvas, selected the paints he needed, and began to put them on the palette.

Once he started painting, the sounds around him vanished. His focus was on the landscape, brush strokes, and canvas. He was ultra-focused for a short while, then soon, he was thinking about Sandra. He continued to paint, but his thoughts were on her.

Was there a way he could make this permanent? She'd said the whole thing was to get him out of her system, but it was like old times all over again.

He should send a text to let her know he was fine and already painting and was thinking about her. Then he thought he didn't want to take up more of her time by interrupting her.

He refocused on his work. For the past several years, Luke had gotten just enough works commissioned to keep him in the black.

He also had a lot of finished work in his canvas bag. Some of his best paintings. He would rather starve than sell them. Once he finished these last two paintings and collected the money, he would have enough to last him a few months, maybe up to a year, if he remained frugal.

If he was really lucky, the guy that ordered this job would commission another set, and he would have work for a while.

The sun made its presence felt. Sweat trickled down Luke's forehead, and he wiped it with the back of his hand. Feeling restless, he fished out his phone from his pocket to check the time. He'd already spent three hours. Time was dragging. He wasn't having fun.

He heard a rumble and looked up to the sky. He hoped rain clouds would gather again from nowhere so Sandra would come to his rescue. But it was only his stomach.

Luke pushed Sandra out of his thoughts. She didn't want him. There was no need to build castles in the air. He was doomed to the life of a wanderer and would be gone once the job was done.

Luke's mind drifted to the home he'd grown up in not far away. Who lived in it now?

Not that many of the kids around moved, but not moving had been one of the most stable things in his life growing up.

Art had been his escape. Clara had said his mother was an artist. Maybe art was her gift to him. Not only did art provide him a way to spend hours and hours alone honing his craft, but it also offered him a way to make money.

In school, the art teacher had mentioned one of the popular websites where anybody could hang their shingle and start offering their services for sale. Luke did just that.

He taught himself Photoshop, signed up to the website, and offered to create two book covers for people at the cost of one. In the early days of indie publishers and eBooks, people jumped on that offer. Soon, he was making decent money for a kid and keeping busy.

That gig eventually dried up as more people got into it.

Luke was grateful for this commission. That was one pressure off his back.

The urge to call Sandra, hear her voice, and know she was fine returned.

Now Luke was worried he was worrying about Sandra. Before returning to Beaver Run, no girl had occupied his mind like Sandra did now. But nobody had taken his cock in her mouth and held him in place until he was spent. Was it lust or love?

He brought out his phone and contemplated whether to send a text or call. He needed to hear her voice. He tapped her name on the screen. The phone rang then went to voicemail.

As Luke contemplated what to do next, his phone buzzed with an incoming text. It was Sandra. She was on her way and would be there soon.

His heart thundered with joy. That was the end of painting for the day. Every slight breeze or rustle in the bushes sounded like Sandra's car driving up the dirt road. He dismantled the easel, put the paints back in the container, and waited.

Just as he finished, Sandra's car came into view. He didn't want to spend any more time out there. He picked up the canvas and easel, and waited for her vehicle to stop.

Sandra got out of the car and walked over to him. She placed her hand behind his neck and kissed and kissed him.

Her lips tasted like nectar. She nibbled his lips. Her tongue darted into his mouth and she pressed her body into his. His jeans tightened right away as he remembered what those same lips had done to his cock last night. He was about to drop the easel and canvas on the ground, grab her waist, feel her up and take her right there on the hood of the car when she pulled back.

Luke stared at her, his breathing fast, chest rising and falling. "What was that for?"

"I don't know," she said breathlessly. "I just wanted to do it. I guess I missed you."

"That makes two of us."

"I brought food." She walked toward the car.

"Thank you. You've been a blessing to me. Maybe we should go somewhere, sit down and eat."

"It hasn't been long I ate. But I can always sit with you." She looked at his hand. "You're done painting?"

Luke nodded and loaded his stuff into the back seat. He looked at her and wanted to kiss her and thank her but wasn't sure how she would see that. Instead, he said, "Was it busy at the restaurant today?"

Sandra bit her lower lips as she did a three-point turn. "Same old, same old. Everybody knew what they're supposed to do." She drove toward the tarred road. Her face brightened. "I have good news for you."

Luke was taken aback. He couldn't fathom what the news might be, but her enthusiasm was contagious. He smiled back. "What?"

"Moe finally picked up your car. I looked in the parking lot, and it was gone."

Luke felt like he'd been punched in the stomach. It was good news, but it sounded like a train wreck. That would bring an end to hanging out with Sandra and take whatever was left in his bank account.

The proverbial shit had just hit the fan.

"That's great. I hope Moe finds out what's wrong with it."

"Moe's good. He might take time, but he gets the job done."

"Is it okay if I eat while you're driving? I'm famished."

"Go for it."

Luke opened the bag and turned to look at her. "Burger and fries. You're a woman after my very own heart."

Sandra laughed.

He stuffed a few fries into his mouth, chewing as he unwrapped the burger. "Come to me, Mama!"

"My God," Sandra said and laughed. "Watching you eat feels like a sexual experience."

It didn't take Luke long to put away the burger and fries. "Thank you, Sandra."

She laughed. "Don't thank me. I'm looking out for myself. Just making sure you have the energy to fulfill your end of our bargain."

"For you, I will call on my reserves anytime."

"I was going to drive to the park so you can eat, but since you've wolfed down your food, do you want to see Moe?"

"Yes, why not."

As they approached Main Street, Luke noticed the ice cream kiosk they used to frequent as kids. He was surprised it was still there. There was a long line in front of it. Sandra loved her ice cream.

At Moe's, he founded out he needed a new battery. That was the good news, but his alternator might be out too.

"Alternator?" said Sandra.

Moe drew a circle with his finger. "The thing that generates electricity for the engine." He turned to Luke. "I'm kind of loaded down," said Moe. "But I'll get back to you as soon as I confirm. As long as you're patient. Your car will come back almost as good as new."

"As good?" asked Sandra.

"Well, considering it has over two hundred thousand miles, it's no spring chicken."

They said goodbye to Moe and got back in the car.

"Where to now?" asked Sandra, tapping the wheel.

"One more stop, and you can drop me off at my place… Stone's place. Oh, I almost forgot. Stone is a nice guy. We had breakfast at Megan's. Then he took me to the sheriff's office. I met Trevor and Clara."

Clara raised her eyebrow. "Did Clara babysit you too?"

Luke swung his gaze to her. "How did you know? She said she knew my mother."

"At one point or the other, she was a babysitter for all the kids in our age group in Beaver Run."

"Maybe I'll talk to her later. What about ice cream? I noticed the kiosk is still open. Can we stop by, my treat?"

"Sure."

They bought ice cream with cones stuck into plastic cups. They drove to the Airbnb and sat in companionable silence as they enjoyed it.

Sandra said, "Do you know you can determine the sex position people love by how they eat ice cream?"

"Get out of here."

"I'll explain. Just holding the cone and licking the ice cream with your tongue. Simple and easy-loves missionary position."

"Plain vanilla."

Sandra nodded. "Those that bite and chew love doggy-style."

Luke growled and winked at her. "Aggressive." He remembered the way she'd offered her behind that night.

"And you…" She looked at him while tapping her lips with a finger.

He'd been licking his ice cream somewhat like the missionary guy, but with almost all his tongue flat on the ice cream and moving his head as his tongue slid up.

"Yep, you love to give head. I can attest to that."

"I love the taste of your pussy. Especially when you sit on my face."

Sandra's nostrils flared out. "Okay, take it easy. That's dirty talk…and it's getting me horny."

"You started it," said Luke. Ice cream dripped down his fingers. "What about those that their ice cream melts and drips all over their hand?"

"The guys love receiving hand jobs. The girls love giving said hand jobs."

Luke stared into space for a second. "Yes, that makes good optics."

Sandra leaned closer. "Do you want to taste mine?"

She'd ordered chocolate while Luke got vanilla. She raised her cone between them. Her tongue shot out and took a lick. Luke did the same. "I knew that!"

Luke shrugged. "Knew what?"

"People that share ice creams also love ménage à trois. Do you want me to invite a friend over? While you eat me, my friend is riding you?"

A shaky breath shot out of Luke.

Every man's fantasy. But a trap.

"No, you're all the woman I need, Sandra."

Sandra smiled like a flower blooming. She shook her head and put the rest of her ice cream upside down in the plastic cup.

Sandra placed the cup on the dash and reached for Luke's crotch. She gasped. "That's a surprise."

Luke was as hard as steel. "At your service, Ma'am."

"I've been your ride all day. It's time for you to be my ride." She unbuckled her jeans and took them off with her panties.

"Shouldn't we go inside?" asked Luke as he opened his fly. "Someone might see us." He pulled his jeans and boxers down to his ankle."

His cock stood like Cleopatra's Needle in Central Park.

Sandra laughed. "You're not even considering your suggestion." She swung her bare legs over him. "I've always wanted to have sex in my own car." Her voice was shaky.

Slowly, Sandra impaled herself on him.

16

Sandra

AS SANDRA DROVE OUT OF THE PARKING LOT TO MEET LUKE, the tourist bus was pulling into the parking lot of Beaver Tail. It was a good arrangement they had going. They stopped by two or three times a week, and so far, so good. Sandra wondered if they were active in the fall and winter months too.

Luke had lived and was still living up to his own part of the deal. The places they had sex was only limited to their imagination. Another exciting place would be her bedroom at her parents' home.

The first painting was already done, and Luke was working on the second painting.

He was now painting from the other side of the lake, and it was a long drive, although from there, you had a good view of the restaurant.

It was also the part of the river her father loved to fish,

which made it risky to pose in the nude there. Her dad could stumble in.

To make matters worse, her father would prefer she had something with Peter.

That was her original plan, but Peter had been relegated to the back burner following Sally's recommendation.

"I could sketch you from my imagination, but I want to see how natural light falls on you in nature," Luke had said the day before Sandra started posing for him.

They'd worked out a plan. Sandra would come right around noon laden with food. They would eat, take a nap, or just sit in her truck and talk.

After that she'd slip into a light robe. Once Luke was set to start, off came the robe, ready to be snatched back if an intruder appeared.

Luke said once he got to a certain point with the drawing, he could work on it without her having to be there to sit for him. She'd sat for a few sessions, and the work was taking shape.

Sandra couldn't believe today was exactly two weeks since Luke had arrived with his beat-up Cherokee and subsequently returned to her life. Sally's suggestion about Luke had sounded like a good idea, but instead of helping wean her off him, she was digging in, falling for him more. It seemed like he felt the same, but she couldn't be sure.

It was like old times when they'd started dating. Maybe things would end differently this time.

The fifteen-minute ride to that part of the town was uneventful. Sandra turned into the dirt road, and as soon as she saw Luke, he stopped painting and walked toward the car.

Luke smiled. "Hi, pretty one."

Her heart did a little jig. Then she remembered this would be coming to an end soon, and her inside tightened.

Relax, Sandra. Enjoy it while it lasts. "Hey."

Luke had on a smile that reminded her of the cat that ate the canary.

"Okay, handsome, spit it out."

"You know me so well. Okay, we have a little company today."

Sandra opened the door and got out. She wore khaki shorts, a button-up flowery blouse, and a light summer shawl. She'd also brought with her a Beaver Tail Restaurant bag.

Sandra raised an eyebrow. "Little company? Like a squirrel, beaver, *Bambi*?"

Luke chuckled. "I didn't mean small in that sense. I meant-"

"Sandra!"

Sandra whirled around and almost dropped the bag. Coming toward her was her father in his fishing gear. "Dad!"

He turned to Luke. "You've been scaring the fish away. All morning I haven't caught anything. Did I have the wrong bait, I wondered? Of course not. I had the right one. I decided to walk off my frustration. Imagine my surprise when I saw your car pulling into the trail. Then I saw him. I know this is not politically correct, but he's not good for you."

"I can hear you, Dad, and so can Luke. We're not invisible."

Her father continued as if she hadn't opened her mouth.

"That's what I'm saying." He stabbed a finger at Luke. "His presence is causing problems. I'm not the only one that thinks he shouldn't be seen. Even the fish agree. That's why they're not showing up." He looked at the easel and made a move toward it. Luke looked around, then grabbed the picnic cloth from the ground and threw it over the painting.

Sandra's father's mouth dropped open. Then he closed it

and swallowed. "Are you that bad you won't even let me see your work?"

Sandra let out a breath. "Phew."

Her father rolled his eyes and shook his head. "Typical! Artists. Always busy but have nothing to show for it." He turned away from the covered painting. "Of course, he can't draw." He waved his hand in disgust. "I'll go back to my fishing."

"Be safe, Dad."

"If it wasn't for your mother, I'd say don't bring him for the barbecue tomorrow."

Sandra heaved a sigh of relief as her father walked away. She turned to Luke. "Thanks for covering me up." She removed the cloth from the painting and scrutinized it. "My breasts are not that large."

"That's what I see. Full, rounded, and succulent." He licked his lips.

Heat rushed to Sandra's cheeks. "Then you need your eyes checked." She paused for a moment. "Why don't you exhibit your work so people can see how talented you are?"

Luke sighed. "You know I work mostly on commission, and most of the work is already accounted for. It wouldn't be fair exhibiting them." He paused. "And we've had this discussion before."

Sandra did remember. It was a long time ago. Maybe it was one of the things that made him leave. She decided not to pursue it any further.

"So what are we going to do? I'm not going to paint you topless with your dad around. He's normally gone by this time. I don't know what happened today."

They stared at the canvas, then Luke said, "I think I can finish the painting at home. Let's leave your dad to fish in peace."

Her eyes not leaving the painting, Sandra said, "You never showed me that sketch of me you did when I was eighteen."

"I didn't? Well, like I said, it's in storage in Mountain Peak."

Sandra pulled her eyes away from the painting and looked at him. "Can we get it?"

"Well, you're driving since Moe has refused to finish my car. Mountain Peak is not that far." Luke combed his hair with his fingers. "We'll have to go to my place and get the key."

Twenty minutes later, Sandra drove as they headed toward Mountain Peak. Luke was kind of quiet. She too felt down. Perhaps it was the inevitability that their arrangement was coming to an end. Or for Luke, going to get the drawing was digging up old memories.

Sandra glanced at him. "Everything okay?"

Luke nodded slowly. "The two weeks seemed to have flown by just-"

"I know! I was just thinking the same thing. That means we were really enjoying ourselves."

"Yeah," said Luke. They drove on in silence.

Suddenly the wail of a police siren started behind them.

Sandra looked at the rearview mirror, then at the dashboard. "Is that for us? I wasn't speeding."

Luke turned around. "Maybe it's Trevor or Stone wanting to say hi."

She got out of the fast lane, and the police car sped past.

Sandra looked at him. "Stone or Trevor…very funny."

"Yeah, I keep on forgetting to ask you about Trevor and Sarah. What's the story?"

"That's Sarah's secret. They met on a train. Trevor was coming back from somewhere…I think California, and saw a damsel in distress. The distress followed them back to Beaver Run. The same problem snagged Stone, and for some weeks, he had total amnesia."

"What? That sounds like a movie."

"Yeah." Sandra saw their turn coming up and pushed the indicator for the right turn signal. "It was all over the papers. Maybe one day, they'll make a movie out of it."

Luke pointed. "You can park over there." He let out a sigh. "I didn't know I'd be coming back here so soon."

Sandra touched his arm. "Luke, we don't have to…"

"No, we're here already. And it's something that must be done. If not today, some other time." He got out of the car.

Sandra walked behind Luke as he led the way to the building, then the lot with his family's stuff.

Luke let out a laugh without humor. "If not for you, I wonder if I would have ever come back here."

He slipped the key into the padlock and unlocked it. The gate opened with a roar as he pulled it up. "I've seen TV shows with rich celebrities having their things in storage auctioned off because of nonpayment. Now I understand. Out of sight, out of mind."

Even though he didn't say it, Sandra felt sadness sip out of Luke as he looked at the piled-up boxes from the home he'd grown up in. He recovered an old dusty duffel bag and then an artwork storage canvas bag placed in a space between two piles of cardboard boxes.

Luke sneezed. "I think it's in here." He unzipped the bag and looked in. "Yep, let's go." He sniffed. "I probably would have to come back again to clean things up for good."

Luke locked the unit, and they left. He carried the two bags.

Sandra's heart was pounding as they walked to the car. "What's in the other bag?"

"Some letters and papers I found in my dad's closet. I didn't have time to look through them then." He smashed the two bags together to get rid of dust before putting them in the back seat. He opened the canvas bag again, rifled through, and brought out the drawing.

Sandra wanted to snatch it, but she couldn't pull her eyes away from his face. He didn't know he was being watched. His lips puckered slightly. A smile tugged at the corners of his mouth. What he was looking at gave him pure joy. Sandra fell for him all over again. "Can I see?"

Luke looked at it and smiled. "Wow, you were an angel. I mean, you're still an angel." His voice was barely audible.

"Give me that." Sandra took the paper, her hands shaking. The paper was thick and smooth, not what she expected. It was a pencil sketch of her torso with her head turned to the side.

"My God, this is beautiful. I looked like a baby."

Luke cleared his throat. "See! Your boobs were perky."

Sandra laughed. "Here, hold it."

Luke held it, and Sandra took a picture with her phone.

He had a proud look on his face. "You've always been a beauty. I'll get it framed."

17

Luke

WITH LUKE RIDING SHOTGUN, SANDRA PULLED UP IN FRONT of her parents' home. "I'll park out here, so we won't be looking for people to move their cars when we're ready to leave."

Good, thought Luke. At least there would be other people to talk to, and not just crazy Mr. Leigh. "Is your dad going to be here?"

Sandra gave him a sideways glance. "It's his house. Just don't mind him. I hope he'll behave himself."

Luke stepped out of the car, and the aroma of barbecued meat hung in the air like a morning fog.

His stomach rumbled its delight. Luke tried to guess what he smelled. Chicken, sausages, burgers? He hadn't eaten all day. He'd been busy putting finishing touches to the painting and saving his appetite. Saliva rushed to his mouth. "I can smell food."

"Dad usually mans the grill with Trevor as his sidekick.

There's Trevor's car. And Stone's too." She looked around. "I don't think Laura's here yet. I can't wait to show her the drawing. In fact, I'm going to hang it in the restaurant."

"With your breasts showing? That's indecent exposure, especially in a family restaurant."

"Nonsense. It's a work of art. Most people won't even know it's me." She walked toward the entrance to the compound.

"I'll tell them," said Luke.

"No, you won't. I'll pay you off." She puckered her lips and pushed her forefinger into her mouth, batting her eyes.

"Sexploitation, that's breaking the law. I'll have you arrested."

Sandra giggled. "Before or after?"

"Ha…good point. Probably after."

Sandra laughed, turned, and continued toward her parents' driveway, with some exaggeration in her steps.

Luke watched her ass swing suggestively from side to side. She wore a blue shirt-like dress that came down to just above her knees, held loosely with a belt. Watching her walking carefree excited him.

Sandra led the way to the backyard. As soon as they walked through the little wooden gate, Luke saw the barbecue setup. Women in summer dresses or shorts, and T-shirts. And men in T-shirts, shorts, and jeans. Some wore matching Bermuda shirts and shorts.

"Sandra and Luke are here!" someone yelled.

It was Trevor standing with Stone.

Sandra raised her hand. "Adela! Sarah!" She raced toward the two women.

Luke smiled and trailed slowly behind her. Aha, now he remembered Adela. She'd filled out to a beautiful woman.

The other girl must be Trevor's Sarah. Sandra and the women hugged.

Luke waved at them. "Hello." The woman he thought was Adela turned to him and smiled.

"I'm Adela, do you remember me from school? Rock... sorry, Stone won't stop talking about you."

"Of course, I remember you," said Luke smiling. "I hope you heard only good things." They shook hands. "Sorry Stone had to leave his place and inconvenience you because of me."

Adela glanced at Stone and back to Luke. "He said that?"

"No-"

"Don't mind him. He loves staying at the farm. Short of selling it, renting it out was the reasonable alternative. We're glad it was of use to you. Otherwise, it would just be empty."

"How are your parents? Mr. and Mrs. Williams?"

Adela beamed. "They're on vacation in Europe. I spoke with them earlier today. They're having the time of their lives." She turned and waved to Sarah. "Sarah, this is Luke. Luke...Sarah."

Luke extended his hand. "Hi, Sarah. Good to meet you."

"Same here," said Sarah and shook his hand.

Luke remembered what Sandra had said about Sarah. She looked so innocent. He couldn't imagine why anyone would want to hurt her.

"Sandra said you just moved here."

"Yes," said Sarah. "And I heard you just moved back."

"Well, not for good. I came to paint. I-"

"Luke!"

He turned to the sound of his name. It was Sandra, and she was dragging her mom.

"Luke, you remember my mom?" said Sandra. A shy smile danced on her lips.

"Mrs. Leigh, of course. Good evening and thanks for inviting me." He extended his hand for a handshake.

"Wow, hello, Luke," said Mrs. Leigh. "It's been a long time." She spread her arms for a hug.

They hugged and patted each other on the back.

"Could you help me thank Sandra? She's been a godsend since I arrived. She's been driving me around, especially with my car in the garage."

Mrs. Leigh dismissed it with a wave. "That's what friends are for. Especially friends that go back a long way."

Luke felt a stab of guilt. Of course, her mother knew how it ended four years ago. He stood there, not knowing what else to say. Sarah, Mrs. Leigh, and Sandra started to talk, and Luke just stood there. What should he do?

Luke felt a hand on his shoulder and turned. "Hey, Trevor."

"Dude, I've come to rescue you," said Trevor. Dressed in shorts and a T-shirt with Garden State and a map of New Jersey printed on it. He looked up in the sky at the fading sun. "I'm sure you're thirsty and hungry. Something to quench your thirst for starters?"

"You bet," said Luke.

"Excuse us, ladies," said Trevor.

They didn't hear. They were engrossed in their discussion.

Trevor took him to a big wooden drum filled with ice and all sorts of drinks. Close by was the grill, next to a table with plastic cups, plates, and cutlery.

On another table were cornbread, salad, dressing, and salsa next to potato chips. Burger and hot dog buns sat next to assorted meats and condiments. Luke swallowed.

Trevor pointed at the table. "Help yourself. Let me know if you need anything that's not here."

Trevor walked off to say hello to Laura and a good-looking middle-aged woman who looked like her mother.

Luke grabbed a plate and made himself a double cheeseburger. He picked up an orange Smirnoff from the ice drum and looked around for where to sit. He more or less inhaled the burger and chased it down with the drink. He went back for seconds, which he consumed more slowly.

Luke, Stone, Trevor, and some other guys that looked vaguely familiar stood around and talked about life in general.

Luke also got to learn more about how Trevor had met Sarah. Then about Stone's amnesia and how he met Adela. They were surprised he'd never seen it in the news.

The sun went down, and crickets started to make their voices heard. Frogs replied with their croaks.

Luke saw Sandra as she lit some Tiki torches and went to help.

"Did you make any new friends?" asked Sandra when he walked up to her.

"Kind of. Everybody's so nice. So what did you decide to do with the drawing?"

Sandra frowned at him then focused on the torch's wick she was trying to light with the lighter. "What do you mean? Like I said, it's going to the restaurant. Actually, I showed a picture to Sally, and Laura and Sally want one just like that. Sally wants you to make her look younger in hers."

Luke wasn't sure he heard right. "W…What?"

Sandra laughed. "You should have seen your face. I was kidding."

Luke heaved a sigh of relief. "I need the bathroom. I've put away three bottles of Smirnoff."

"Come on, I'll show you. I've only had one strong Margarita."

As they walked into the house, Luke saw Sandra's dad. He hoped the man would look his way so he could wave, but he didn't.

"Right there," said Sandra.

Luke locked the door. He sighed with relief as the golden shower hit the porcelain. He shook himself dry, washed his hands and checked himself out in the mirror, liking what he saw.

Luke opened the door and was about to step out when Sandra pushed him back into the bathroom. She locked the door and stared into his eyes.

"What's going?" asked Luke.

She silenced him with a kiss. Her tongue probed his mouth.

Luke yielded. His tongue slipped into her mouth and engaged hers in a fencing match.

Her hands slid down into his shorts, fondling and squeezing. Soon his pride and joy stood erect and hard.

Luke pulled back, breathing hard. "Sandra, somebody might come…"

"Not before me."

Luke chuckled. She was on fire, and he knew he couldn't reason with her. His only hope would be to speed things up. He hitched up her dress, squeezed her behind, then ran his finger along the elastic band of her underwear to the front. He slipped his hands in and cupped the tuft of pubic hair he encountered. His two fingers slid down and curved into her pussy.

Sandra shuddered. "I love the way you grab my pussy."

"You're so wet."

She whimpered. "It's all your fault."

Luke burrowed his fingers deeper.

Sandra let out a shaky breath, hot against his face. "Yes,

that feels good, deeper." She removed her hand from inside his underwear, unbuckled his belt, and undid his buttons.

In one swift move, Sandra pushed his boxers down to his ankle. She sat on her haunches and licked her lips as she watched Luke's cock dangle like a fireman's hose in front of her.

Sandra grabbed his cock by the base. "So big. So beautiful." She tapped her forehead with his shaft like a baton.

Luke stared down, his mouth open and his chest rising and falling. His whole body was waiting for the fantastic experience he knew was coming.

She licked her lips, then traced the head of his cock with her lip and guided it into her mouth.

"Oh yes, Sandra," said Luke as the warm wet cavity engulfed his pride and joy.

She bobbed her head back and forth and hefted his balls in her other palm, rolling and squeezing gently.

"I like the way your lips wrap around my cock." Excitement shot through Luke like a bolt of lightning straight from his cock to his brain. Sandra worked his dick harder.

Luke threw his head back and sucked in air. "Baby, you are a cock whisperer."

"I love the way you feel in my mouth. Are you going to come for me?"

Her words hitched him onto the cum express lane. Luke felt bombarded by sensation, then came a loud knock on the door.

Boom! Boom! Boom!

18

Luke

THE SOUND DERAILED LUKE. WHO COULD IT BE?

Sandra pulled his cock out of her mouth with a pop. Then she pushed it back and ran her tongue from the base of the back of his shaft to the tip. She yelled, "Occupied!" as she motioned for him to sit on the toilet cover.

Luke did as he was instructed.

Once he was in position, Sandra stood astride him. She raised her dress with one hand, and with the other, she shifted her panties to the side, positioned his cock, and lowered herself onto him.

Luke groaned. "Yes." He felt her wetness wrap around his cock. Like sticking a finger into warm, thick, hearty oatmeal.

Sandra lifted herself up and slammed down on his cock. "You like that?"

He didn't trust himself to speak and nodded vigorously. His hands found her butt cheeks. They felt good in his hands-round and juicy. He went to work, lifting her up and lowering her down onto his cock.

Luke wondered for a second if the porcelain throne could hold their combined weight. As Sandra lowered herself onto him and clenched her pussy muscles around his shaft, jolts of pleasure swept through him. He just couldn't think. He kicked that door shut.

Sandra rose and fell, making little whimpering sounds, twisting, and turning. Looking for the right position for maximum sensation.

Luke knew when she found it because she took him to the hilt, did a grind, then gradually increased speed. She moved faster and faster, moaning and groaning, chasing maximum pleasure.

Luke held on to her ass, trying to keep his cock buried deep inside her. She moved as fast as the pistons in an engine oil commercial on TV.

Sandra was grinding and riding him faster and faster. The slap, slap, slap of skin against skin reverberated in the half bathroom, urging him on.

Luke's eyes were on her face. Her eyes were shut tight, her mouth the shape of an O, nostrils flaring with each gasping breath. He, too, felt the excitement building up deep inside him.

"I'm coming, I'm coming." Sandra's voice was a whisper.

Luke held on for dear life. He, too, was swept up into that frenzied climb up the hill.

Her pussy fastened around his cock like a vise. Her mouth opened wide in a silent scream. Then her face relaxed. Her breathing came in gasps.

Sandra whimpered, then went limp, wrapping her hands around his neck, her face buried in his chest.

Luke dug his fingers into her butt. He buried his face in the crook of her neck.

His breathing came in gasps and he roared as his orgasm ripped through him, "San...Sandra, I love you. I love you so much." He couldn't help himself.

She shivered against him. "I love you too."

Boom, boom boom!

They both jumped. Someone banged on the door.

"Do you need help?" asked a female voice.

Luke sucked in air. "No!" he yelled. "Can't someone take a dump in peace?"

"Oh, sorry," said a low voice from the other side of the door. "It's not my fault you're constipated."

Sandra got off him. "Luke..." She rolled out some tissue and wiped herself. "Are you constipated?" She managed a smile and gave him some tissue. "You leave first. I have to pee."

Luke nodded. He washed his hands, splashed cold water on his face, and dried it with a paper towel.

Behind him, he heard the sound of Sandra's pee-it was a strong stream from the sound of it. He looked himself over in the mirror and nodded.

"I'll be in the garden," said Luke and turned to look at Sandra. Her head was angled up, her lips full, eyes glazed. His eyes lingered on hers. Luke felt something in his heart right at that moment. Something he couldn't describe.

Sandra pursed her lips and crinkled her nose. "What?"

Luke lowered himself and kissed her lips. It was slow, then it built up to a frenzy. He'd kissed her so many times, but this time it felt different. His whole body was on fire again as if he wanted to possess her to be one with her.

Sandra was on her feet now.

Luke drew back, then kissed her once more on the lips.

"Meet me in the backyard, okay?" He brushed the hair away from her face.

Sandra nodded. "Okay."

He stepped out of the bathroom, hearing the door lock behind him, and he walked briskly to the exit and went outside.

The evening was humid and now dark, the garden lit up by strategically placed tiki torches.

"Will You Still Love Me?" by Chicago blared from the speakers on the porch. It seemed like Peter Cetera was talking to him directly. He headed for the drum with the drinks.

The smell of barbecue and accelerant hung in the air, reminding him of other happy times he'd had at the beaches out in California some years ago. People stood or sat in groups talking and smiling.

Something had changed inside that bathroom. When Sandra looked at him, he'd looked away for no reason at all. He couldn't be shy. And he'd told her he loved her.

God, was it love he was feeling? *Jesus, Luke! This was just for fun. You can't be falling for her.*

He got to the drum with the drinks and was surprised it was halfway down. He dipped his hand into the freezing mixture of water and ice and brought out the first thing he touched. A bottle of Corona beer. He twisted the cap off and took a long drink.

The cold beer cooled its way down his inside.

Luke welcomed it. He took another swig as he looked around. A lot more people had shown up.

He saw Sandra walk out of the house, and his breath caught. His heart started to beat faster. It was like time stood still. She was beautiful.

A young man walked up to her. He must have called her

name because she turned, and her face brightened. She was all smiles and hugged the guy.

Luke's grip on the bottle tightened. He didn't like the way the guy was looking at her.

"Luke, Luke."

It was a female voice. Luke turned around to see Laura standing with her mom, waving him over. Next to them were Trevor, Mr. Leigh, and another man.

Luke walked up to them, smiling. "Hello." Laura's mother looked elegant in her ankle-length sundress.

"I'm Sally Paterson, Laura's mother…"

"It's a pleasure meeting you, Mrs. Paterson."

"Please call me Sally. I'll cut to the chase. I'm the librarian, and we're having an exhibition at the library. We'd be honored to have some of your artwork to display. Ummm, no nudes, please. Especially of young girls we know."

Laura's eyes widened. "Mother!"

Luke smiled. "Oh…Can I think about it?"

"Sure."

"Luke! There you are."

It was Sandra's dad. His face was flushed. He looked like he was responsible for the drum with drinks being almost empty.

"Excuse me," Luke said to Laura and Sally. "Mr. Leigh calls."

Sally chuckled. "Nice meeting you. Think about the exhibition."

"Good evening sir," said Luke when he got to the group. "And thanks for having me."

"I heard you're done with the painting."

"Good evening. Yes sir. I just finished."

"Right, so I presume you're leaving soon?"

"Ummm…yes."

Sandra's dad beamed. "Awesome." He turned to the man beside him. "He's been painting Sandra, distracting her. He won't even let me see the painting."

"Come on, Dad," said Trevor. "They are old friends."

His dad waved him away. "Once he leaves, she can focus on Peter." He directed his gaze ahead and smiled. "Look at them. Peter and Sandra do make a nice couple."

Luke followed his gaze. What he saw was like a kick to his crown jewels. Sandra and the guy he'd seen her with earlier were deep in conversation.

19

Sandra

SANDRA CLEANED AND TIDIED UP HER PARENTS' HOUSE before heading home. She recalled the events of the night in her head as she drove and shook her head. Love songs played on the radio, but she barely heard them.

Looking for Luke had started out as a joke. After she came out of the bathroom, she was still basking in the euphoria of what just happened.

She'd gone straight to the kitchen and drank water. Her mother came into the kitchen with some friends, and they all chatted. Then she headed outside.

She saw Luke by the container with the drinks, remembered what they just did, and goosebumps covered her skin from head to toe. Something had changed between them inside her parents' bathroom. It was like finding religion. Believing without seeing.

Sandra had wanted to have him in her childhood bedroom

to fulfill a teenage fantasy. But '*opportunity comes once in a lifetime,*' according to the rapper Eminem, and she took it.

She must tell him how she felt before he skipped town. He'd said he loved her. Maybe that was why it was different this time. She felt it. They were older too.

Sandra exhaled. She would go to him, take a moonlit stroll, and talk things out. She took the first step, and Peter appeared from nowhere.

"Hello Sandra," he said and grabbed her hand.

After what seemed like an eternity, probably minutes or less, Sandra was finally able to disengage from Peter Chett, his father, her own dad, and Trevor. Luke was nowhere to be seen.

She asked around, subtly, not wanting to draw attention to her predicament. Laura said she'd seen him a minute ago by the drinks container.

Sandra called his cell phone. Her heart was pounding so hard she thought it was going to jump out of her chest.

"Hi," said Luke. He sounded breathless.

Sandra felt an unexpected release of tension. A slow smile parted Sandra's lip. "I've been looking for you."

The reply from Luke was heavy breathing.

"You sound out of breath… Where are you?"

"I'm jogging home," said Luke.

Sandra knew he could run and hold a conversation at the same time. Back then, when he told her about it, he called it running at your conversational pace. Good for long distant runners. Helped with stamina.

"Why? We came together, right?"

"Well," said Luke. "I didn't want to break up the conversation between you and your beau's family."

Then she understood; he was jealous. A smile had crossed

her lips. She'd been going to him after she came out of the house when Peter accosted her and wouldn't quit talking.

Sandra was annoyed with her father too. He kept on insinuating that Peter and she were a couple in waiting.

He shouldn't be making plans for her behind her back. In fact, he shouldn't be making plans for her period.

Maybe things would have taken off with Peter if Luke hadn't waltzed into town. The smile on her lips faded.

"Sandra? Are you there?"

"Luke…it's not what you think. I-"

"Let's talk about it later." Luke cut her off. "Holding the phone and running is uncomfortable. I don't have my earpiece."

"Okay, I'll call you later." She hung up.

That was about two hours ago. Sandra volunteered to help with cleaning up and told Trevor to hit the road.

It was late when she was finally done. Her parents had retired for the night.

Sandra let herself out after turning on the home alarm. Her whole mood was sour, and she felt sticky and dirty. She needed a shower. Instead of calling Luke, she sent him a text.

Luke replied he was almost asleep. *See you tomorrow?*

She replied *Okay*.

The digital display on her dashboard read 1:00 a.m. as she drove home. A thought occurred to her, and her car almost came to a dead stop. Did Luke overhear her father talking about her and Peter making a good couple?

She could hear her father's voice. *Good riddance to an artist that can't draw.*

Sandra nodded unconsciously; he must have. Something had happened to her too in that bathroom that she still couldn't get a grip on. Then it hit her. It was like a repeat of when they were in high school when he sketched that nude drawing of her. She'd fallen in love all over again.

Luke was the kid without a mother who everybody was sorry for, but glad it was him and not them.

Sandra never thought of Luke as a potential date until she saw him drawing in art class.

She fell in love with his skills. Then he volunteered to draw her and was bold enough to touch her in places where no one had. He had her from the first pencil sketch.

Seeing her house pulled her out of her reverie. She was home, sweet home.

Sandra pushed the indicator for the right turn signal and drove into her driveway.

She was scared. Luke was going to leave again-she knew that. Tears trickled down her cheeks. He'd said he loved her when his cock was buried deep inside her, and he came hard.

Sandra believed his response was an emotional knee-jerk reaction. The excitement-the danger of getting caught making out with the hosts' daughter right under everybody's noses.

For her, it was a different story. She was in love. An affection that wouldn't be returned. The tiny chance they had was now gone, destroyed by her father and his flippant remarks.

Sandra wiped her eyes with the back of her hand. She'd been parked in front of the garage for God knows how long. She pushed the button for her garage door to open.

Sandra drove in and pushed the button again to shut the garage. She turned off the car but remained inside listening to the whine of the pulleys as the garage door came down.

Sandra was shocked by this revelation. Looking back at it now, the outcome of her decision to have sex with him at all times was obvious. For most women-for Sandra, sex wasn't a detached performance. The best experiences, the best orgasms she'd had, were always coupled to love. And they were all with Luke.

Should she tell him the whole thing? That she was sowing her wild oats, but her heart betrayed her? No, he would only laugh at her. Maybe not to her face. In his mind, it was just another free pussy.

Sandra turned up the volume of the radio and listened to 106.7 FM playing romantic songs. How long she stayed inside her car in the garage, she couldn't say.

But when "Another Sad Love" song by Toni Braxton started to play on the radio, Sandra decided it was time to get out of the car. The song summed up her love life.

"No," she said out loud.

She wouldn't let the pain she felt the last time Luke left consume her again.

Sandra was a big girl. She would disengage from him, and they would part as friends this time.

Luke never made her any promises. She wouldn't act hurt even though her heart felt like an old wound had been reopened and was bleeding again.

20

Luke

Dogs howled and barked as Luke sped past homes in the dead of the night. Not wearing sports attire, he was sure he looked like a thief escaping from a burglary gone wrong.

He hoped someone would call the cops on him. A night in jail would be a good distraction from where his mind was going.

Luke ran from Sandra's parents' home. He had planned to sprint all the way, expend his frustration on running. He would fall asleep from exhaustion and spare him the pain of thinking about what he saw.

Sandra had called him, but he didn't break stride. He took the call while still running and found out she'd been looking for him. They spoke a little and then hung up.

Luke ran for another ten to twenty minutes before arriving home unmolested by dogs or concerned citizens.

He stopped in front of the door, hands on his knees,

inhaling and exhaling, his whole body moving with each heartbeat.

Sweat poured down his face as if he had a small, angry rain cloud above his head. His lungs burned. Each breath he drew in felt like inhaled fire.

As his breath returned, Luke went from a stooping to a standing position. Sweat had dripped from his body and pooled on the cement floor in front of the door.

In his heart, Luke knew he felt something, but it was no use. Sandra was already moving on with her own plans. Her whole family was on board. He'd really made a fool of himself coming to the get-together.

Maybe it was a good thing he saw in plain view Sandra's plan all along. No wonder her father was always belligerent toward him. Peter was who he was rooting for. Luke had come in from nowhere and almost spoiled things.

Luke was done with Sandra. Knowing was better than not knowing. He won't feel encumbered to make his own decisions.

He would let Bill Madden know it was time to come pick the paintings. Once that was done, and he collected his money, the contract would be officially ended.

He would be in a better position if he had another commission before signing off on this one. But he needed money too to pay Moe for his car.

Luke hated the vulnerability he felt whenever he was out of money. The insecurity was always debilitating, and thinking about it now, it had always been there. In a sense, history was about to repeat itself. He must find another job before ending this contract with Bill Madden.

Luke didn't know much about Bill, except that he was a shrewd businessman who commissioned works in batches from artists who he felt were up and coming. He'd keep the art, and hopefully, in the future, when the artists became famous, he would sell at a higher price.

Luke shivered as a gentle breeze caressed his skin, bringing him back to the present. The air was warm, but all the sweat on him was evaporating, chilling him.

How long had he been out here thinking? His clothes were wet and cold. He was no longer sweating.

Balancing on his left foot, Luke bent his right knee. He grabbed his right ankle, pulled toward his butt, and held it for ten seconds.

He felt the stretch on his right thigh muscles. He did the same for his left leg while balancing on his right foot.

When he was done, he dug into his pocket, retrieved the key, unlocked the door, and went inside.

Luke turned on the shower to heat up and took off his wet clothes. Once the water was comfortable, he went in and adjusted the shower head to tiny pinpricks like in Sandra's bathroom.

The warm water and the spray jet helped calm him down. By the time Luke got out of the shower, clean and smelling of bodywash, he was ready to begin planning for the next steps in his future.

Sandra was already a lost cause, he thought as he dried himself.

He stopped toweling as the realization hit him. He'd succeeded in the task he and Sandra agreed to. He'd actually given so much of himself to her that she'd had enough.

She was now ready to move on with this shit or Chett guy, whatever his name was. He'd fucked her so much that she didn't want any more of him. He was out of her system.

Luke cocked his head. "Hmmm, imagine that."

He smiled and resumed drying himself. The irony of life,

he thought as he stepped out of the shower and onto the bathmat to dry his feet.

The smile faded from Luke's lips. He was supposed to be neutral, not fall for her. She'd met her own goal, and he'd just gotten trapped. She wouldn't believe him if he said he loved her. After all, he couldn't be trusted. Once bitten, twice shy.

Luke changed into his sleeping clothes. There was no need crying over spilled milk. He fell in love when he was not supposed to. He would let his subconscious figure things out while he slept.

Tomorrow morning, he would work the phones. If everything else failed, he would call on Mr. Baltimore. A few years ago, he'd wanted him to make a few paintings for him, including the Hollywood sign. That would be his last resort if all failed. Tomorrow would be a busy day for him.

Luke was almost lost in sleep when he heard the buzz of an incoming text. It was from Sandra. His cock jumped.

Was she coming for one last time? He'd read somewhere that when you find a woman that excites both your loins and your heart, she was a keeper. But she wasn't for him.

Luke sent her a reply. He was almost asleep. See her tomorrow.

21

Sandra

IT WAS MONDAY MORNING, AND SANDRA FELT REJUVENATED. She'd woken up early, ran, showered, and now drove toward Luke's place.

The day before, Sunday, she'd overslept. And when she awoke, a text from Luke was waiting for her. He said he was putting finishing touches on the paintings to get them ready for delivery. She had planned to visit him, but that text had cooled her heels.

Maybe he was swamped, but it could also mean he was already disengaging and didn't want to see her. Either way, she also needed time to sort out her feelings and stayed away.

This morning she'd sent a text as soon as she got in her truck telling him she was on her way. Luke had replied immediately. *Come right in, the door will be unlocked.*

Sandra's girly parts twitched. She wondered what she would say when she got there. Bring up the events of the barbecue night, and talk about Peter? Or pretend nothing happened?

She believed she owed him an explanation. Her father did not speak for her, and nothing was going on between her and Peter.

With that out of the way, they could then continue with whatever he had in mind by leaving the door unlocked. Maybe then she would tell him how she felt.

She drove to Luke's place, parked the car, and let herself in. She smelled coffee. Sandra made a mental note to get some later, then headed for the bedroom.

She knocked softly, then opened the door to the odor of fragrant masculine bodywash and the sound of the shower.

She froze. A pair of blue jeans, a white button-down shirt, and a navy-blue blazer were laid out on the bed. On the floor was a pair of brown Dockers. A knot in her stomach tightened. Was he leaving already?

She knocked on the bathroom door. "It's me. I'm here!" She hoped he could hear her over the sound of the shower.

"Sandra! Sandra!" His voice was muffled.

"Yes!"

"I'll be in here a few more minutes. There's fresh coffee in the kitchen. Help yourself."

"Okay!" said Sandra and walked out of the room. She took deep breaths to calm herself.

In the kitchen, Luke's phone sat on the kitchen island connected to a charger.

Sandra needed some coffee to calm her nerves. She opened a few of the kitchen cabinets before she found the one with mugs. She made herself a cup. He was definitely going somewhere, but where?

With her coffee mug in hand, Sandra walked to the living

room and noticed the canvas bag with his paintings was wide open. She decided to check them out.

Sandra put down her coffee and looked through them. She recognized some of the paintings from their days in college.

Sandra smiled. "Wow!" The beach in Atlantic City, a flower vase, a deer looking at the painter…she continued to look through the canvas frames.

The paintings were all beautiful. Sandra couldn't believe he still had them. Working artists create art to sell, not to keep. Maybe she should tell him about the exhibit at the library. He should put some of them out there. You never know.

A piece of paper fell off one of the canvases as Sandra moved it. She picked it up and noticed it was an ATM receipt.

She didn't want to look at it, but curiosity got the better of her. She opened it and frowned. The account had ten dollars in it. "What?" Sandra muttered to herself.

Luke's phone started to ring in the kitchen. Should she get it? It might be important.

She looked at the receipt again. It was from two weeks ago, the day he'd arrived. He was broke.

The phone started to ring again. Sandra put down the receipt and rushed to the kitchen. As she reached for the cell phone, it stopped.

She let out a sigh of relief. She didn't really want to answer. Then the house phone started to ring.

Sandra didn't worry about that. Probably someone looking for Stone. She was still trying to figure out what to do about the paintings when Stone's cheerful voice came on and asked the caller to leave a message.

The caller apologized for calling Stone's land phone and began to leave a message.

Sandra knew that voice.

It was Moe. Of course, he knew Luke was staying at Stone's place.

He said he left a message on Friday and just now on his cell phone. He said the car was ready, told him the amount, and he could come and pick it up at his earliest convenience, and hung up.

Unless Luke had another bank account, he didn't have money to pay Moe. What was going on?

Sandra cocked her head. Did she hear something outside? She walked over to the window and peered out.

A black town car idled outside behind her car. Luke was indeed going somewhere.

"Hi, Sandra."

She whirled around.

Luke stood there, tucking his white button-down shirt into his jeans.

"Hi. You startled me. There's a car out there-"

"Yes, it's my ride to the airport," said Luke, looking down and tugging at his zipper.

"To…to the airport?" stammered Sandra. Her insides froze. For a second she felt faint and dizzy, like the essence of life had been sucked out of her. She took a deep breath.

"I was on the phone a lot yesterday. This guy wants me to fly over to California so we can finalize some work he wants me to do for him." He looked up. "Are you okay?"

Sandra touched her brow. "Yes, I'm fine." She forced a smile. "Just need more coffee." But she wasn't fine. He was leaving again.

Luke buckled his belt and threw out his hands, palms open. "All expenses paid. So I said why not?"

"You could have asked me to drop you."

Luke jerked his thumb toward the cab. "Remember, all expenses paid."

Sandra remembered the call. "Oh, your phone was ringing earlier, then the house phone. It was Moe…he left a voicemail. You want me to pay him and get your car for you?"

Luke hesitated. "No, that won't be necessary. I'll take care of it once I get back. I'll call him and let him know." He walked back to the room and, moments later, came out wearing the blazer.

Sandra felt it was already too late for them. Luke was working on the next phase of his life. He had already made his next move. They could still part as friends.

"Hey, there's going to be an exhibition at the Beaver Run Library," Sandra said. She pointed at the canvas bag. "I could put some of your paintings up there and generate some interest."

Luke paused. A flash of anger crossed his face. Then he smiled. "Sandra, it's not necessary. Moreover, Laura's mom told me about it already."

"Exposure. You have to put your talent out there, Luke- sell some paintings. I was looking at them. Some are from years ago."

"Don't worry about me. I don't have any problem selling my work. I'm going to California to close a deal. Worry more about your Peter."

Sandra's jaw dropped. So she was right.

Luke picked up his leather messenger bag and walked over to her. "I overheard your dad at the barbecue talking about his wishes for you and Peter."

She wanted to tell him how she felt. It had started as a fun thing to do, but she'd fallen for him again. But her lips wouldn't move. She wasn't going to beg.

"Anyway, I have to go." He leaned forward and kissed her on the cheek. "Lock up and keep the key. Or leave it under the flowerpot. I'll call, okay?"

Sandra nodded. "Okay, have a safe flight. When are you coming back?"

"I don't know yet. Maybe a few days. I'll call." He walked out and shut the door.

Sandra drew in a deep breath and exhaled through her mouth.

Suddenly the door burst open. Sandra jerked.

Luke rushed in, a worried look on his face. He looked around, then dashed to the kitchen. He came out with his cell phone. "Nearly forgot it." He smiled at her. "Bye again, and thanks for everything."

Sandra heard voices, then two doors slamming. She walked to the window and watched as the driver backed out and drove away.

She sat on the couch. This was déjà vu all over again. What was she going to do? Her mind drifted to that morning four years ago. She'd gone to visit him at his apartment off-campus. He'd made his plans without telling her.

If she hadn't come to visit, he would have left without telling her or saying goodbye. She'd felt like an old rag, used, and discarded.

And here they were, four years later, and the same rag had been dusted up, used, and discarded again.

Sandra blew air into her fist as if she were trying to keep warm. He shouldn't be blamed. The plan was all hers, and he'd gone along.

She got up and looked around, not sure what to do next. Well, she'd have to get back to the restaurant. Her eyes fell on the paintings again. Luke wouldn't be having money problems if he sold some of them.

Without thinking, she took the nude of her they'd picked up from storage and the landscape of Beaver Run woods, the one without the nude figure. It still smelled of paint.

Unbreak Her heart

She would show the world his talent even if he didn't want to. You don't light a lamp at night, then cover it with a bucket.

She would frame the pencil sketch and mount the landscape's stretched canvas on the wall in her restaurant. The reception area would do just fine, so anyone coming in would see it.

Sandra locked the door, put the key in her purse, and left.

She drove straight to the Glasses' gift and flower shop. Mary, Mrs. Glass, was in.

"That's a beautiful drawing," said Mary in her slow squeaky voice. She held the sketch down at the four corners with paperweights.

"Thank you."

Mary pursed her lips. "Hmm, she kind of looks familiar. We'll choose a mat. That's the border around the image, so it draws attention to the young girl." She brought out a bunch of L-shaped mats and placed them close to the image. "What do you think?"

Sandra wasn't sure what to do. "You're the expert. I trust your recommendations."

"Okay." Mary placed another mat close to the image, looked at it, and nodded. "Where are you going to put it?"

"At the restaurant, close to the reception area."

Mrs. Glass nodded. "Non-glare glass would be perfect so people can see it without the reflection." She brought out a long ruler and measured the paper. "You're in luck. The size is standard. We don't have to custom frame it. We already have precut glass, frame, and mat."

Sandra couldn't contain her excitement. "How long will it take?"

"Well, if you can drop in at Megan's for coffee, maybe

some pancakes, eggs, and sausages, I'll be done by the time you finish. Like in twenty minutes."

"Twenty minutes?"

Mrs. Glass nodded.

"I'll wait then." Sandra rushed off to Megan's next door. She ordered, took a seat, and waited.

Sitting there when she had her own restaurant made her uneasy. When her order was ready, she ate in her car.

Sandra walked into the gift and flower shop some thirty-five minutes later, and the job was done.

Mary said, "Mr. Glass worked on it." She unwrapped it and showed Sandra.

Sandra beamed. "It's beautiful."

As Mary wrapped the frame in brown paper, her husband walked in from the back. His hair was gray, his spectacles at the tip of his nose, and an apron over his shirt and pants.

"Good morning," said Sandra, smiling. "Thank you."

Mr. Glass's eyebrows shut up. "Hello!" His lips widened in a big smile grin. "You're welcome."

Sandra walked toward the exit with the package.

"It's her. It's her!" Mr. Glass whispered loudly.

"That's some good tits."

Heat rushed to Sandra's cheeks. She continued walking, but she could still hear them.

"Men!" said Mrs. Glass. "Is that all you saw? What about the beautiful face?"

"What? Oh yeah, that too," said Mr. Glass.

22

Luke

LUKE LOOKED OUT OF THE WINDOW ON ROUTE 15 ON HIS WAY to Newark Airport. He didn't notice the parade of trees and cars, nor his reflection on the window. All he saw was Sandra Leigh.

How beautiful she'd looked when he walked out of his room and saw her in the living room, her blond hair in a ponytail and a blue summer dress that stopped above her knees, showing off toned calves. All he wanted to do was take her in his arms and whisper sweet nothings into her ear.

He wanted to be with her forever, as they had planned those many years ago before he'd screwed it all up.

Until Luke saw her two weeks ago, he thought he'd forgotten her, but seeing her on his first day back to Beaver Run had rekindled feelings he'd buried.

The look on her face less than an hour ago when he told her he was traveling was the same look she'd had when he left four years ago. That look had haunted his dreams and made his heart bleed. Yet he'd gone and done it again. She stood there, like a deer caught in headlights, her thoughts paralyzed by the juggernaut pain crashing inside her.

She shouldn't have been surprised when he mentioned Peter. She had a life before he showed up. But yet she was. Why?

Luke was surprised from his observation on Saturday and, by Sandra's dad's account, how far her relationship with Peter had already gone.

But she'd come to him again and again without reservations. Was there more to it than met the eye? Was Sandra's dad interpreting things differently?

She had offered herself as a model for him to paint. A Joan of Arc to the rescue, and threw in free pussy to boot.

When he heard her father at the barbecue dismiss him as a mere distraction, he'd felt used.

Now looking back, it seemed like Sandra had set up an elaborate scheme to get back at him with the hope he would fall in love with her, and then she would yank the rug from underneath him. Leaving him exactly the way he left her?

Luke shook his head. He'd fallen for it-hook, line, and sinker.

Glancing around, Luke noticed a sign for the airport and remembered seeing that same sign years ago. That first assignment he'd gotten right before graduating was, funny enough, in California too.

One wise man said that history always repeats itself. Only the fool doesn't learn from it. Today was his turn to play the fool.

Luke had spent a year painting sandy beaches all over California. Carmel-by-the-Sea, a city in Monterey County, was his favorite. It was a place favored by writers and artists with picturesque streets, houses, and beaches.

At the end of that year, he hadn't made much money, but his skills had developed a great deal. He always painted on commission and also made paintings of scenes that intrigued him in his spare time.

He'd never sold any of those special paintings. They were like old friends.

His thoughts drifted to Sandra again. He remembered telling her he loved her in a moment of passion. Feelings he'd guarded behind a solid wall had spilled out. He was glad she didn't bring it up. She probably saw it as the babbling of a man overtaken by lust.

His thoughts drifted to what could have been if they'd stayed together those lost four years. Would they be married? Living the American dream with two kids, a dog, and a house surrounded by a white picket fence?

Maybe. That thought warmed his heart.

Traffic slowed, and Luke's mind drifted back to why he was on the highway and where he was going. The euphoria he felt quickly faded as the reality of where he was as of today hit him.

As far back as he could remember, he'd always wanted to draw and paint. As a kid exploring their basement, he had discovered sketch paper, all types of pencils and paint, and started to draw. Drawing and painting came naturally to him. When it came time to make a career decision, it was easy: art.

But he hadn't reaped the benefits. Now looking back, the advice given by guidance counselors that people should follow their dreams and do what they love seemed overrated.

He had followed his dreams, and instead of getting ahead, he'd run around in circles. Now he was back to his starting position—literally.

He was in back Beaver Run, broke, loveless, not loved,

and older. In the grand scheme of things, he had nothing to show for his life.

Granted, he'd completed a few pieces, gotten a few commissions here and there, but never enough to get him to where he wanted to be. That now begged the question, where did he want to be? And what did he want from life?

Outside, traffic started to move. Soon the driver took the ramp for the exit to the airport.

Was he making another mistake moving away instead of staying put and fighting? Luke didn't think so. This time it was obvious that Sandra was going for someone else.

He would stay in the loop, but it seemed like the odds were stacked against him.

23

Sandra

SANDRA, DRESSED IN KHAKI PANTS AND A BLOUSE, WALKED into Beaver Tail from the back entrance. It was Tuesday morning, and the day looked promising.

The smell of bacon, fried onions, and peppers reminded her she needed to put something in her stomach too. She checked her cell phone as she headed for her office. There was nothing from Luke, only a text from her mother. She would call her later.

Luke had sent a text when he arrived at LAX yesterday, and since then she hadn't heard from him.

Sandra dropped her bag in the office and then headed for the restaurant's reception area, where she'd hung the pictures.

She stopped briefly at the kitchen and said hello to the chef.

"Good morning," said the hostess with a big smile when Sandra walked up to her.

A college student that lived in Mountain Peak, she'd been with them all summer and had learned the ropes fast.

Sandra looked at the drawing behind her. "Anyone commented about them yet?"

"Well, yesterday, some of our regulars looked at them as if they knew something was different but couldn't figure out what."

A smile tugged at Sandra's lips. That was a start.

"But today!" said the hostess, throwing her palms out. "On my God, it's a different story. They're like, oh, you guys have new paintings of…" She looked down, smiled as if she were about to say something not pleasant, and caught herself.

"Don't be shy. What else did they say?"

"They kept on asking who the girl in the nude was? Whether it was me," she blurted out and laughed. Her cheeks and neck turned red. "I wish I had that type of body." She looked at the picture. "The look on her face is both happy and flirtatious. Like she's in love, but not sure."

Sandra glanced at the drawing again. She always marveled when different people see and feel different things while looking at the same piece of art.

Should she tell her that was her in the painting? Sandra decided against it. Speculation added to the intrigue.

"Oh, there's a gentleman in table eight. Smiles a lot and is wearing a suit. He comes in every now and then for lunch. He looks important, like from the government or something." She nodded in the direction of the table. "He said to let him know once you come in."

Sandra's eyebrows narrowed. Who could it be? She looked at table eight, glad the hostess knew to use the table number instead of pointing.

Sandra relaxed. She turned to the hostess. "You're right. It's the mayor."

Her hands flew to her lips. "I didn't know." Her voice was a whisper.

"It's all right. I'll go see what he wants."

As Sandra approached table eight, the middle-aged man dressed in a light gray suit touched his napkin to his lips, put it down, and got up. "Sandra."

"Mr. Mayor. Good to see you!"

"Sandra, the pleasure is all mine. You look great, as always. The food here was good. Now it's fantastic since you took over."

"Thank you." Sandra left it at that. It was just polite talk. Even though Beaver Run was a small town, elected officials acted the same, whether in Washington, DC, or Beaver Run- always kissing ass.

Sandra had heard the same went for police stations. They have the same feel worldwide, no matter the country.

The mayor beamed and patted his stomach. "Not good for my waistline, but I can't stay away."

"We always put our best foot forward," said Sandra. Nothing had changed in the kitchen in Beaver Tail. It was still the same chef. "I hear you wanted to see me."

The mayor gestured at the chair opposite his. "Yes, yes. Please sit. I'll only take a minute of your time."

He took his seat as Sandra sat. Palms up, he swayed gently from side to side as if trying to figure out the best words to use to say what he wanted to say. "I noticed the new paintings…"

Heat blazed under Sandra's collar. Did he know it was her? Would she be reprimanded? "Ummm…yes. I put them up yesterday."

The mayor beamed. "I recognize the landscape. It's a view of the woods and lake."

Sandra let out a breath she didn't know she was holding. "The landscape?"

"Yes."

"Oh, yes! It was done by a local artist-"

The mayor's eyebrows shot up. "Get out of here! Who?"

"Well, he grew up here in Beaver Run, then moved out. Luke, Luke Martin."

"This is the first time I'm seeing his work. He's good." The mayor took a sip of his coffee, then rubbed his hands together.

Oh, oh, thought Sandra, *the shoe hasn't dropped yet.* It must be the nude he really wanted to talk about.

"He did the nude too?" asked the mayor, the smile gone from his face.

Sandra nodded cautiously. "Actually, yes." She would defend it as a work of art. There were centuries-old paintings of naked women in the Louvre, in Paris, for Christ's sake.

"Well, it's good news it was done by a son of Beaver Run. We have a huge empty wall in the municipal building, and a work like that would fit in nicely."

A knot tightened in Sandra's stomach. No way was she going to put her naked portrait in the municipal building. She maintained a poker face.

"And considering it was done by an artist that grew up here, it would make an excellent conversation piece and would be featured on the town's website too." The mayor paused and exhaled. "The long and short of it is, is there a way the town can acquire it? We'll pay market price."

Sandra couldn't believe her ears. She didn't know what to say. "It's…it's on loan to me from the artist. I…I could ask him…"

"Okay, that would be great." He looked at his watch. "I'm hosting a meeting with the county mayors in the next couple of hours. I have to go. Let me know as soon as possible." He got up from the chair and extended his hand.

Sandra got up, and they shook. "I'll get back to you as soon as I can."

He gave her a genuine smile, pushed his chair into the table, and headed for the exit.

Sandra watched him, and it occurred to her this was exactly what she had in mind-exposure. Luke wouldn't mind, or maybe he would. But what he didn't know wouldn't hurt him. "Mr. Mayor?" She walked fast toward him.

The mayor turned. An eyebrow shut up. "Yes?" He gave her the politician smile.

"What's on the wall now?" asked Sandra.

He shook his head. "Nothing. It's bare."

Sandra blurted out, "I'll bring it over…on loan to the town. I know he won't mind." Then she added quickly, "I'll let him know, of course. He'll be back in a few days, and we'll take it from there."

The side of the mayor's lips crinkled before he smiled. "That would be lovely. Thanks so much, Sandra."

This time she knew his smile was authentic. Sandra walked with him to the exit. After he left, she glanced at the painting and the drawing again. Things were working out better than she'd anticipated.

Sandra went back to her office, literally floating on air. She took the inventory clipboard and went around the restaurant. She checked the walk-in pantry, humming as she went, taking notes.

"Someone is happy today," said Chef Cletus when Sandra waltzed into the kitchen to check the freezer. "I'll have whatever you're having."

Sandra beamed. "Hi, Cletus." She nodded and continued to the freezer.

She opened the door, and a blast of cool air caused her to shiver. Her skin broke out in goosebumps. Sandra looked in, wrote on her notepad, and shut the door.

With that done, next was the smaller kitchen pantry, her last stop.

Sandra returned to her office and woke up her computer with a shake of the mouse. She started to order the inventory they were low on.

Luke drifted back to her mind. She picked up her cell phone from the table, and the screen lit up. No missed calls or texts from Luke or anybody.

He wasn't supposed to keep her updated-they were not dating, but this news involved him. Luke must know the mayor loved his artwork. At least that should put a spring in his steps, if nothing else.

"Oh gosh, the mayor." She'd completely forgotten. He must be waiting for the painting. She put her computer to sleep and rushed to the reception area.

A few people with cameras hanging down their necks, wearing all types of hats and caps, loitered in the reception area.

Tourists. Most were dressed in shorts and wore T-shirts with words like *I love New York, Jersey Girl,* and *Lady Liberty* printed on them. They stood around the reception area admiring the paintings—*the new paintings*.

Sandra's pulse started to race. She saw Mr. Murphy, big and imposing, wearing a Yankees baseball cap and matching Bermuda shorts and shirt.

"Ah Sandra! There you are," he said in his deep commanding voice. "I see you've added some new artwork to your collection. They, are *very* nice."

Sandra willed herself not to blush. What was she thinking? That people wouldn't know it was her in the drawing. "Thank you."

"The hostess was just telling me it was done by a local artist. Does he have a studio or an exhibit around here?" He motioned with his hand. "My group is interested in seeing what else he has." He paused and took a step closer to the wall. "Are you by any chance looking to part with the lovely unclothed Mona Lisa? She kind of reminds me of someone."

Unconsciously, Sandra folded her hands over her chest. Heat crept all over her body. She opened her mouth to speak, but words deserted her. Her eyes darted to Mr. Murphy, then away.

"I can see you're reluctant to part with it. Does the artist have a portfolio?"

An idea came to Sandra in a flash. "Hmmm…there's an art exhibition at the library tomorrow."

Mr. Murphy's forehead furrowed. "Which library?"

"Oh, Beaver Run," said Sandra. Her voice got stronger as she saw the possibilities. "I can convince Mr. Martin, the artist, to put up some of his work there."

"Tomorrow?" Mr. Murphy took off his hat and ran his hand through his hair. He put it back and stroked his chin. "Okay, tomorrow then."

Sandra almost jumped up with excitement. "All right. See you guys tomorrow, about this time?"

Mr. Murphy looked at his watch. "Yes, eleven should work."

Sandra walked Mr. Murphy and his entourage to the door. Once they left, she took down the landscape painting and rushed off to the municipal building.

Sandra couldn't believe it. In less than twenty-four hours of exposure, Luke's artwork was getting so much attention.

She needed to do two things: ask Sally, then get permission from Luke.

She dropped off the landscape painting with the mayor's secretary and rushed over to the library.

Sally was on her lunch break when Sandra arrived, eating at her desk. Perfect timing. Sandra went straight to the point.

"Luke is the one you are rocking his world, right?" Sally waved a hand in the air. "Don't answer that. I already know. I saw the way his eyes followed your every move at your parents' home. You've rocked his world."

Sandra pretended she didn't hear, hoping the heat spreading through her wouldn't give her away. "So can I bring them?"

Sally's eyebrows shot up. "He changed his mind. I told him about the exhibition at the barbecue. He didn't sound interested."

Sandra threw up her hands, not sure what to do. "Typical Luke. He probably didn't see how it would move his career forward. I already have people interested, and they're scheduled to be at the library tomorrow."

Sally sighed. "It's very likely he'll say no if you ask him." She thought for a moment. "You know what? Bring what you can. He's like 99 percent of men out there. They don't know what's good for them, especially when they're getting it for free."

24

Luke

LUKE HEADED TOWARD THE AIRPORT EXIT. HE KNEW A CAR would be waiting for him. It was a long flight, and sleep had eluded him. But he looked forward to meeting Mr. Baltimore again, the millionaire art collector who had ironically given him the commission four years ago that got him started.

Luke should thank him for commissioning so many landscapes for him to paint. It was like paid learning while he perfected his skills.

But no thanks because the job took him away from Sandra.

He'd sent a quick text to Sandra after the plane touched down to let her know he landed.

He'd last seen her six hours ago, and he already missed her. The time they'd spent in her parents' home flashed through his mind. The smell of her hair, her smile, his palms cupped around her firm butt, lifting her up and down on his shaft. He felt a stirring in his loins. Was this love, lust, or a combination?

He looked around, expecting someone to be watching. Nobody was. Everyone was minding their own business, hurrying to their destinations.

Thinking about her made him question himself again. Was he making the right decision leaving Beaver Run now that he had a reason to stay? He quickly reminded himself it was financial and that she had Peter.

Was she spending time with Peter? He clenched his teeth and pushed that thought away.

The smell of coffee and an assortment of other foods caused his stomach to rumble. For the moment, it was a good distraction from thinking about Sandra. He kept on going, planning to grab food on the way to the hotel or before he met up with Mr. Baltimore.

Luke knew he shouldn't be having financial bottlenecks based on the quality of work he produced. Putting out his work would get more people to look at it. But his father would have killed that for him.

Luke remembered vividly in seventh grade when he showed his father a painting he made that came first in the school's art competition. His father had barely glanced at it before tossing the paper to the side.

Since that day, Luke never went out of his way to show anyone his work.

But his work must be better than good, at least for people like Mr. Baltimore to want to work with him.

Luke chuckled. "Because you're cheap, asshole," he muttered under his breath.

Mr. Baltimore was a businessman first, interested in getting Luke's art at a bargain. He made his millions from trading in commodities. Buying low and selling high.

Sometimes he kept the commodities in storage until such a time, due to one reason or the other, when demand outstripped supply and prices shot up astronomically. Then he would sell and make a tidy profit. That was precisely what he was doing with Luke's artwork.

Luke had walked to the exit. A line of men and a few women stood close to the door. A middle-aged man in a black suit held an iPad with Luke's name written across the screen. Luke approached the man.

The man's eyebrows shot up. "Mr. Martin?" he said in a faint British drawl. It was more of a confirmation than a question.

Luke smiled. "Yes."

"Mr. Baltimore is my employer. Do you have any checked luggage?"

"No, this is it." Luke raised his carryon. "I can carry it."

"Very well, sir. This way, please. Mr. Baltimore is expecting you."

Luke followed him. It crossed his mind that maybe this man wasn't who he said he was. That he was about to kidnap him. Luke grinned at that thought. Of what use would he be to anyone?

Luke realized the man had stopped walking and stopped. His thoughts were interrupted when the back window of a Cadillac Escalade beside them came down.

"Luke!" said a gravelly, hoarse voice.

Luke knew that voice ravished by years of booze and cigarette smoking. He turned and peered into the wrinkled old face of his benefactor. His leathery skin had a permanent tan, and he looked even older than the last time Luke had seen him. Luke was sure the man was approaching a hundred.

Luke smiled. "Mr. Baltimore, good to see you."

"Same here. Glad you came. Hop in." He made a sign for Luke to walk round to the passenger side.

Luke handed his bag to the driver, who placed it in the trunk.

Luke got in the car and turned to face the old man. "So what is the theme this time around?"

Mr. Baltimore's eyebrows shot up. "Theme? That's a good way to put it." He raised a finger. "One second… Charles, to the Griffith Observatory, please."

"Yes, Mr. Baltimore," said Charles.

Mr. Baltimore continued, "Well, I'm thinking of America's important landmarks and monuments, starting with the Hollywood sign."

Luke nodded. There were many monuments in America. One man's heap of sand could be another man's monument. He let out a deep breath and looked out of the window. People in New Jersey and California were dressed alike at this time of the year.

"Thinking about it?"

"Yes, I'm just wondering if you'll need an artist with the same caliber as Andy Warhol. And landmarks would become the artist's version of Warhol's Campbell's Soup paintings."

"Well, maybe. But when Warhol made them, he wasn't that famous. Those soup cans literally made him. We'll start with the Hollywood sign, if you agree. That's where we're headed to right now." Mr. Baltimore chuckled. "In the future, your painting will be known as Luke Martin's Monuments."

Luke liked the sound of that. But, at the end of the day, he'd be creating art for someone else at a low price. Again, Luke thought of his future.

He could increase his price per painting. After the Hollywood sign, he could opt to paint the Statue of Liberty, so he'd be closer to Sandra. Then he remembered she already had Peter.

"It sounds interesting," said Luke.

Mr. Baltimore nodded. "Good."

They arrived at the Griffith Observatory about forty-five minutes later.

The massive white building on the south-facing slope of Mount Hollywood housed an observatory, an exhibit hall, and a planetarium.

"So will you do it?" asked Mr. Baltimore. His eyes were on Luke.

They were in the observation deck of the observatory.

Luke glanced at the Hollywood sign. "It's beautiful." He chewed on his lower lip then walked toward the guard rail along the edge. He stood there for a moment, then walked back to the millionaire.

"I can see you're struggling with this one," said Mr. Baltimore.

"Yes, it took fourteen years and almost a billion dollars to finish Mount Rushmore-"

"There's no rush." Mr. Baltimore raised his hands, palm facing forward in surrender. "Excuse the pun. Think about it and get back to me. I just wanted you to see the magnitude of the project."

"I can't get closer to the sign, right?"

"Protected by law. Trespassers are arrested."

Luke was dropped off at the Hilton hotel close to the airport about an hour later. He promised to get back in touch with Mr. Baltimore as soon as he reached a decision.

He bought two Snickers bars from the vending machine to take the edge off his hunger. Once in his room, he ordered room service.

When the food came, a tuna sandwich, Luke ate.

The infusion of calories got his brain working again, and he realized there was nothing really to think about. He'd made the trip in the first place for financial reasons. He was out of money.

Luke dozed off and woke about three hours later. He checked his phone-nothing from Sandra. His finger hovered over the screen to call her.

But that would make him pathetic, considering where her heart was. Luke killed that thought, then jumped into the shower.

With no deadline hanging over his head, he had time to spare. But he had this nagging feeling he was missing something. About thirty minutes later, he rode the elevator down to the lobby.

Luke had a few friends in Los Angeles from years ago when he worked for Mr. Baltimore but decided not to contact them. This was 'me' time. He'd just have dinner and call it a night. He took an Uber to a Mexican restaurant that served the most delicious chicken fajitas with sour cream he'd ever tasted. They were still there.

After dinner, he saw a movie and did not think of Sandra four two hours.

Luke returned to his room after the movie and ordered two Seagram's wine coolers. They should help him sleep.

Noticing his cell phone battery was low, he got his charger from his overnight bag, unplugged the table lamp, and plugged in his charger. It buzzed twice—one for connecting to power and the second, a text from Sandra.

Luke sat on the bed and started to read. She'd had a busy day. She was about to call it a night and hoped things were working for him as planned. She said she would talk to him tomorrow. He reread it. It sounded dismissive.

"Whatever."

Luke sighed, tossed the phone on the bed, and went to the bathroom. He showered, changed into a blue extra-large T-shirt and black and gray checkered pants.

Propped up with pillows on the bed, he drank wine and watched TV. He was one of those people who alcohol made more introspective. He drained the wine and placed the bottle on the nightstand.

Despite the wine, sleep didn't find him. Luke tossed and turned with thoughts of losing Sandra forever on his mind. He plugged in his earphones and opened the app for deep sleep brain waves with ocean sounds. It didn't take long after that for sleep to claim him.

The following day, sunlight streaming in through gaps in the curtain woke him. He thought he would have a definite answer for Baltimore, but he didn't. If he said no and Baltimore canceled his ticket back to New Jersey, he would be stranded in LA—unless…

The unfinished word hung in the air like an eagle on a hot summer day. "Oh shit!"

He jerked up to a sitting position. At the same time, his phone chirped-an incoming text.

"Shit, shit, shit!" How could he have forgotten?

Luke felt like he'd just been rung up on a busy grocery store cashier line and discovered he didn't have his wallet. He felt his balls tighten.

He read the text. *Just got off the plane. Will call as soon as I'm in the rental headed your way, Bill.*

How did he forget Bill was coming today? *Duh, that was the reason you had two weeks to finish the paintings in the first place.*

Bill was supposed to come to Beaver Run in two weeks to pick up the paintings and release the funds held in an escrow account for Luke.

The contract was straightforward: ten paintings in exchange for the money in escrow.

Luke needed that money badly. He sent a text to Bill to meet him at the Airbnb address.

Luke exhaled. Nervous laughter escaped his lips. They had some stipulations in the contract, which Luke thought were silly then, but he had signed anyway. Now out here in California six hours away, his worst nightmare was just about to be realized.

There was no way he could catch a flight in the next few minutes and meet Bill in an hour.

He would have to call Sandra and ask her to collect the paintings from his place and bring them over to her restaurant. Then he'd direct Bill to Beaver Tail Restaurant to pick them up from her.

Luke picked up his phone. He prayed Sandra would agree to help.

25

Sandra

SANDRA HAD A BUSY DAY IN FRONT OF HER. SHE NEARLY skipped her morning run but reasoned it would be an hour well spent.

If she blew it off, the extra hour gained wouldn't make much difference to her day but negatively affected her mindset. She didn't need negativity.

Once done with running, Sandra hit the shower.

Dressed for success in a dark gray skirt and button-down light blue shirt, she set off for Luke's place. Sandra hummed as she drove and gave herself a pat on the back as to how successful her idea of displaying Luke's artwork had become. People noticed it right away.

Sandra's mind drifted to last yesterday evening when the mayor's secretary had dropped in at the restaurant to eat and sought her attention.

The secretary wore a black skirt suit, white blouse with more than enough buttons undone to show off her ample cleavage. She seemed to be on a high from dealing with all the dignitaries from their county-level meeting.

The secretary beamed at Sandra, then attacked her food like the plate was speed dating and would be getting up soon. "The mayors and their entourage gathered to admire the painting during a break." She rolled pasta with her fork, speared a meatball, and guided it to her mouth. She chewed quickly, then swallowed. "The artist's name is Martin, right?"

Sandra nodded.

"I'm positive he'll be getting painting orders soon from all the mayors that attended. They all wanted something similar."

Sandra was delighted. "Really?"

"Mm-hmm."

The buzz of an incoming text from her phone pulled Sandra from her reminiscing. She picked it up and put it on the magnetic knob on her dash. Sally was reminding her to drop off the paintings at the library as early as she could.

Sandra sent a voice text. "Will do."

Minutes later, she stopped in front of the Airbnb and let herself in with the key.

Warm air and the smell of stale garbage ushered her in. Wrinkling her nose, she went to the kitchen and cranked open the window overlooking the sink. Fresh air rushed in.

Sandra opened the lower cabinets one after the other until she found garbage bags. She removed the old one, tied the neck off, and double bagged it with a fresh one, then put a fresh one in the can.

Sandra washed and dried her hands, then went straight to the canvas bag with the artwork. She looked at the partially open paintings and right away saw her dilemma—which ones to take and how many.

She unzipped the canvas bag, exposing the wooden rack

inside with paintings in every slot. It looked like the bicycle parking rack in front of the library.

She wondered how many paintings were there and decided to count. She was at number nine when a text came in. Using her finger as a bookmark placed on the ninth painting, she looked at her phone.

It was Sally. *Where R you?*

Sandra let out a groan. "Oh God." Sally seemed more interested in this than she was. "I'm coming," she muttered out loud.

Sandra didn't know which ones to take. She grabbed the canvas bag and carried it to the back seat of her truck. She came back to the house, picked up her purse, and locked the door.

Her phone buzzed again as she pulled the key out of the lock. Sandra dropped the key as she reached for her phone. It clattered to the floor. Now running late, she raised one side of the flowerpot and kicked the key under it. She headed for her car and tapped the screen to call Sally.

"Where are you?" asked Sally.

"Hi, Sally, good morning," said Sandra, hoping she didn't sound annoyed. "On my way."

"Did you get the paintings?"

"Just."

"Good. Drive to the back of the library when you get here. I'll let you in."

A few minutes later, Sandra drove into the parking lot. It was empty except for Sally's car parked all the way in the back. It reminded her of coming to church early with her parents and siblings as a kid.

In the next three hours, this same place would be filled with cars and the town's white municipal bus picking up and dropping off senior citizens like clockwork.

At 7:30 a.m., the Beaver Run Library, a stone's throw from the sheriff's office, looked like a cemetery as Sandra pulled up beside Sally's car. She glanced at the old oak tree next to it. Birds and butterflies flew around the leafy branches.

A plaque by the main entrance, which Sandra had seen a thousand times, told the institution's story.

The library began as a place for children to aggregate under the branches of the red oak tree to be told stories. They were children of the first migrants, mostly miners and fortune seekers from Europe more than two hundred years ago.

Now the building housed about ten thousand books in a climate-controlled setting. The children and adults were protected come rain or shine by the building instead of the tree.

Unless some man-made calamity befell the place, Sandra expected the tree and building to be here for another hundred years.

The back door creaked open, and Sally stood there all smiles. "Come in, come in. Do you need help?"

"No, I'm good," said Sandra as she rushed to the back seat of the truck and grabbed the paintings. She followed Sally in.

The smell hit Sandra first. A faint moldy odor peculiar to old basements mixed with the smell of old books and a dash of sewer stench. The door led into a wide, well-lit space with bookshelves loaded with books lining the wall.

"He painted all those?" asked Sally as she led the way up a wide staircase.

"There's still more. I just grabbed the first ten."

"Ten is a good number to start with."

Sandra got to the top of the stairs to the main library floor.

"Wow, it looks big and feels different when you come in through the back door, and there's nobody here."

Sally shrugged. "Hmm, it feels the same to me. I always come in through the back door."

Sandra looked at Sally, noticing her makeup, large round glasses, and white blouse over a long black skirt. She'd gone for that sexy librarian look depicted in magazines and described in books. She couldn't help herself. "You went for that sexy librarian look, eh?"

Sally twirled around and almost tripped on her high heels. She steadied herself. "I can't wait to get off these heels. I wonder how you young girls stay on them all day?"

"But you don't have to wear them."

"Are you kidding me?" Her husky, deep voice rose to a higher pitch. I'm going for Mrs. Robinson from *The Graduate* look. Your friend Laura and I can pass for sisters-who know what tourists that bus of yours might drag in. I have to look my best."

Sandra's nose flared. She looked around, then remembered nobody else was around.

Sally extended both hands to take some of the paintings. "Okay, let's see if that lover boy of yours can really paint and draw. Or whether he did his best work because he wanted to impress you and get into your panties."

"Sally!"

"Don't Sally me. Throughout history, love, and the promise of sex, have inspired men to achieve way beyond their capabilities." She put the canvas on the table and looked at them one after the other.

Sandra's eyes were on her face. Sally didn't speak, but her facial expressions spoke volumes. She was impressed. She said nothing until she was done with all ten.

Sally's voice trembled when she finally spoke. "My God, Sandra, he's got skills. Okay, let's go put them up."

Sandra was amazed by how much preparation Sally had done. The exhibit was in the quiet section of the library. An easel with a square whiteboard had text on it that read *Local Artists Exhibition.*

"I have to get more tripods. Ten paintings, right?"

Sandra nodded.

"I'll get four more." Sally headed for the stairs.

"Do you need help?"

Sally emphasized no with the wave of a hand and went down the stairs.

Sandra looked around. There were other watercolor paintings from local artists and even a children's section. But nothing compared to the ones she'd brought in. Did she bring a lot? She didn't want to intimidate the others.

Sandra whirled to the sound of wood clicking against the wall. Sally appeared carrying easels. "You should have called me to help you."

"Yeah, I should have. Anyway, I'm here now." Sally put them on the table. "Just straighten the legs. I'll arrange them."

Sandra grabbed one, assembled it, and put it down. She picked up a second one then cleared her throat. "I was thinking, maybe having so many paintings from one person is intimidating and not fair to the others. Maybe I should take some back."

Sally's head shot up straight. "You'll do no such thing! Of course, it's intimidating. His work is excellent. I just wish I'd invited more people."

Sandra lowered her head to hide the big smile on her lips. She picked up another easel. "Okay." She wasn't the only one that his work appealed to.

They were done about fifteen minutes later, and more of the library staff drifted in.

"I'll have to get to the restaurant," said Sandra. "I'll direct Mr. Murphy over or bring them myself depending on how free I am."

Sally nodded. "Sounds good."

Sandra said hello to some of the library staff that had wandered over to look at the paintings. Two of the male library staff admired one of the paintings. Out of curiosity, she inched closer and took a look. Heat cascaded through her body. The nude in the woods with her rounded breast in full view and her face in side profile caught their interest.

26

Luke

LUKE SAT ON HIS BED IN THE HOTEL ROOM, HUNCHED OVER his phone. Thoughts jumbled up in his head like different colors from several paint tubes, squeezed onto a palette, and mixed with a brush.

Eventually, all that tumbling mixture of colors would blend into one smooth new vibrant color. That was precisely what Luke wanted his brain to do.

Luke believed his new vibrant color, the solution to his predicament, was there. It was just for his mind to move things around and latch on to it.

Sandra's smiling face wondered into the mosaic his mind was creating. He let out a breath and felt his body relax. She completed him. What was she doing right now? Was she with Peter? He forced that thought out of his mind. Happy thoughts only. He needed a clear mind.

Luke turned to the sound of two clicks and a hum. Then

straw-colored blinds billowed as the gusts of air hit them from the AC vents.

Moments later, Luke felt the coolness on his face like tiny drops of mist from a spray bottle.

His voice drifted back to Sandra again, and he called out her name. "Sandra." His voice was low. Was he doing the right thing moving away from her again?

Well, this time, she was the one pulling away and not because of a job, but because of a man. Even if he wanted to ask her to give them a chance, he felt it was already too late.

But for now, they were still friends, and she could help him. He wanted it to remain that way.

Luke's mind snapped back to his predicament, and a plan started to take shape. He had to get back to Beaver Run as soon as possible. His first task was to confirm a ticket on the next available flight back to Newark. Then contact Baltimore, Madden, and Sandra by text.

He confirmed his flight through the airline's app.

Holding his phone in a horizontal position between his palms, his thumbs went to work. Both thumbs struck the screen fast as if he were sending telegrams on steroids.

Luke chuckled. Text messages are the telegrams of the twenty-first century.

Next, Luke typed up a text to Mr. Baltimore. He was likely to accept his offer, but they would have to amend the fee structure.

Luke figured that would buy him time while he collected money from Bill. With money in his pocket, eliminating a desperate mindset, he could put his foot down on a higher fee structure. He hit send.

He rolled his shoulders, took a deep breath, exhaled, and started to type a text to Bill.

Bill Madden was a shrewd businessman. Born and bred in

Chicago, there was a huge disconnect between his love for art and the roughness he exuded. He didn't appreciate art the way Mr. Baltimore did. To him, it was all about profits.

Dressed in a three-piece suit most of the time, Bill Madden looked calm and sophisticated, but once he opened his mouth, it was all glitter, no gold. Other people that commissioned art would put some money down first, but Bill had wanted to pay when the work was done and he liked what he saw.

At first, Luke didn't like the idea, but just like now, he'd needed money. He sighed. Things change, but somehow, find a way to remain the same.

Luke had sold one of his paintings then. He'd been living off of that and by being very frugal. When he sold that piece, it had felt like giving up a part of himself he would never get back.

He'd made a promise to himself never to part with any of his uncommissioned works, no matter what, after that.

He and Bill had agreed to put the funds in an escrow account. Luke had also insisted that the money for the ten works be placed in the account. Bill threatened to walk away but later changed his mind after adding his own stipulations.

He would walk away if there were any delays or the job was incomplete by the agreed-upon date.

Bill then said, "It would be like putting money under a mattress for a rainy day, but without fear of a fire or rats getting to it."

Luke agreed. He'd never missed a deadline.

Luke's text to Bill now was to disregard the first text and follow the new one. He instructed him to go to Beaver Tail Restaurant and ask for Sandra, the manager. She'd hand over the ten paintings after he released the funds.

Luke then sent a text to Sandra.

With his marathon texting done, Luke took a deep breath and let it out through his mouth. If only he'd thought about this yesterday, he would have taken the red-eye out of LAX and not involved Sandra at all.

The differences in time zone between New Jersey and California would have worked in his favor.

Luke looked at the time on his phone. His flight was in an hour and forty-five minutes. He gave himself roughly thirty minutes to get to the airport, then through security.

The battery on his phone was low. Luke was about to hunt for the lightning connector charger when he saw it sticking out underneath the blanket.

He plugged it in and rushed into the bathroom. Good thing the airport was nearby. He had a plane to catch.

Seven minutes later, Luke retrieved his phone and cursed. The lightning connector belonged to the headpiece, not the charger.

He dressed quickly-jeans, a T-shirt, and a blazer from yesterday. He threw his toiletries bag and dirty clothes into his bag, slipped into his Dockers, and rushed downstairs.

He dropped his card key at the reception desk, and as he inquired about the complimentary hotel shuttle to the airport, was told one was just about to leave.

Luke hopped on it.

En route, he powered on his phone, and it advised him to go to low power mode. Luke muttered under his breath and booked a cab for his trip from the airport to Beaver Run. He memorized the confirmation number just before his phone died.

Forty minutes after leaving his hotel room, he stood in the security line.

He made it just in the nick of time to board his flight.

27

Sandra

SANDRA FINISHED WITH SALLY AT THE LIBRARY AND DROVE straight to her restaurant. Out of habit, she looked toward the spot where Luke's car had been parked. Hopefully, Luke would pick it up from Moe once he got back.

She wondered if her broken relationship with Luke would ever be fixed, but deep down, she knew this was it.

Sandra parked her car and checked her phone. There was still nothing from Luke. Her heart felt like it was shrinking from watching love desert her again. Sandra wore a cheerful face as she entered the building, even though she knew her efforts might not be appreciated.

She looked into the kitchen. "Hi, Cletus."

Cletus smiled. "Hey! Mr. Murphy mentioned they'll be coming for an art exhibit today at the library."

Sandra smiled. "He did?"

"Yeah, he said he'll bring a few new friends. His friends won't travel for pancakes, but they'll travel to look at art."

Unbreak Her heart

In her mind, Sandra hoped they wouldn't be disappointed. "Sounds great. I just dropped off the work with Laura's mom. I hope they won't be disappointed."

"Hmm, don't worry about that. Art is subjective. Sometimes I look at some pieces from Picasso and how much they're worth, and I just shake my head. Now when you talk of the masters like Da Vinci and Michelangelo, who basically created photo-quality images by hand, then I agree with the high worth."

Sandra laughed. "I know what you mean. Anyway, I'm going to be in the office for a while. If they get here before I'm out, please let me know."

"Will do."

In her office, Sandra got to work. She'd already ordered what they were low on. She checked through the tan-colored folder marked receiving to see what had come in yet.

The beverages usually arrived first.

She checked them off.

Next was scheduling. Apart from people like Cletus, whose schedules were like Swiss watches, she would have to talk to each person and find out if there were any specific days they wanted off. It was a pain, but she'd rather have it all figured out before making the schedule.

Sandra finished a bunch of work in her office and wondered when Mr. Murphy and company would show up. Then there was a knock on her door.

She waited for a moment. People knocked, then popped their head in. She waited, and when that didn't happen, she said, "Come in." It was probably one of the summer hands. The hostess looked in.

"Sorry to bother you, Ms. Leigh…"

Sandra smiled. "Hey there. Come on in."

The girl came in and shut the door. "There's a guy out

there dressed in a three-piece suit. He asked if you were here. And I said let me check."

Sandra was surprised. "It's not the mayor or one of his people?"

She let out a nervous laugh. "At least I know he's not the mayor. He could be one of his people. He looks official, but there's something different…"

Sandra looked at the wall clock in her office. "Wow. Time really flies."

The hostess glanced at the clock, then back at Sandra with a knowing smile. "Yep. Those are the best hours when you're so busy and you're not paying attention to the time."

Sandra got up and walked toward her. "He's at the hostess station?"

"Yes."

"Okay, I'll walk with you. So what about the bus? It's like they're running late today."

"Oh, the group?" The hostess turned and frowned. "No," she said, shaking her head slowly. "They were here. They came in, ate, then left." She looked at her watch. "About an hour ago. There were a lot more people. I overheard them talking about going to the library."

For a brief moment, Sandra felt like she couldn't get enough air. "Cletus-"

She stopped herself. He must have been busy and forgot. They walked across the restaurant toward the front.

"I'm actually on my lunch break, but I can come along if you want."

Sandra patted her on the shoulder. "No, go along. I'll take care of it." She continued to the front toward the visitor. She would have been more comfortable if the hostess were with her.

Sandra took a deep breath and approached the hostess station. She felt apprehensive, like one time she was pulled over by a cop in New York. She hadn't been speeding but felt like something was going to go wrong. Or that she had done something she wasn't aware of. It turned out one of her rear lights wasn't coming on when she hit the brakes.

Sandra saw the man admiring the photos and painting on the wall, his back to her. She could tell from the fit of his suit that it was bespoke.

He must have heard her approach because he whirled around.

He had close-cropped blond hair and a nose that looked a little crooked. Maybe broken a few times. The man could pass for good looking but for his eyes. They were cold and dark and danced up and down Sandra's face.

"You must be Sandra Leigh. I recognize Luke's work." His voice was smooth like aged wine—someone used to the art of persuasion.

His head darted from her to the pencil nude. A smile creased the corner of his mouth.

Maybe it was not such a good idea leaving the drawing there in the open after all, thought Sandra as the back of her neck simmered.

She waited for the second shoe to drop. A remark about her breasts or something.

Sandra smiled. "Yes, I'm Sandra…and you are…?"

The man extended his hand. "I'm so sorry. I forgot my manners. I'm Bill Madden. Please call me Bill. Luke said I should ask for you. You should be in possession of some ten pieces of artwork…"

Sandra extended her hand, hesitated then shook his hand. "Artwork? Luke?"

"Yes. I was supposed to meet Luke today," said Bill. "Well, he sent me a text this morning to meet you instead."

Sandra was confused. "He's in California. He didn't... He sent you a text this morning?" Sandra hadn't checked her phone since she came back from the library. That was three hours ago.

Bill nodded.

"You said about ten pieces?"

Bill smiled. "Yes, landscapes."

Sandra raised a finger. "Can you just hang on...let me check my phone." Her eyes darted around, and she noticed an empty table. "Please." She pointed at the empty table, her heart hammering in her chest. "I'll grab my phone." She motioned to one of the waiters by the bar to come over. "What can I get you?" She handed him the drink menu.

Bill took it, and without looking at the menu said, "Iced sweet green tea with lemonade."

"Sure," said Sandra and nodded at the waiter, who smiled and wrote it down.

"I'll be right back," said the waiter.

Sandra hurried off. Could Luke have planned all this without telling her? Back in her office, she went straight to her handbag, rummaged through, and found her phone. She pushed the home button, and her phone came on. Beep after beep came from it as soon as she turned it on, and messages started coming through.

Her breath caught as she looked at the list of text messages and missed calls. "Jesus." It must have been out of signal range while buried in her bag.

There were texts from Cletus, Luke, Sally-she clicked on Luke's first. He said he was on his way back from California. He'd sent a Bill Madden to meet her. He was sorry for the inconvenience.

Don't trust him. He also sent a link to an escrow account website plus the username and password. Sandra was not to hand over the paintings before Bill signed off that everything was satisfactory. She was to hand over the landscape nude plus nine other paintings. Ten in number. All the ones before a blank white canvas in the large bag.

A shaky breath rushed out of Sandra. Her throat went dry. There was no place to hide.

She felt the same way she had a few years ago as a New York waitress bar, helpless and scared, when a drunk had smashed through the bathroom door while she was peeing, with her panties around her ankles.

Luckily one of the waiters saw him the first time he threw himself at the door and came to investigate. As soon as he knocked down the door, he was on him, pulling him away.

One of the landscapes was in the mayor's office.

"Oh God," said Sandra. A whimper escaped her throat. That she could quickly get back. But the nude and a bunch of others were in the library. Sandra realized that she and Sally had not talked about what would happen when a customer showed interest in a painting. A shaky breath rattled out of her.

Hands trembling, Sandra called Sally. "Pick up, pick up." It rang through and went to voicemail. She called again and again, and each time it went to voicemail. She had to go to the library and retrieve them. She would tell Bill to give her a few minutes.

Sandra took a few deep breaths, squared her shoulders, and walked into the restaurant toward Bill's table. She plastered on a smile she hoped was convincing. Her inside felt like Jell-O.

"You're right. My purse acted like a Faraday box, keeping the signal away from my phone."

Bill raised an eyebrow. "Everything all right?"

"Yes. I had a few messages from Luke. I'll go bring the pieces. Please enjoy a meal with our compliments while I'm gone. I won't be long."

Bill winked at her. "I'll take you up on that offer. I'm hungry."

Sandra gave instructions for him to be served whatever he wanted and dashed off to her car. The smell of chemicals and heat rushed out of the car once she opened the door.

The rest of the paintings. Sandra hoped heat hadn't damaged them. She remembered when she'd started to count the artworks, there was a thin blank canvas she'd encountered. That was the separation mark. She had taken everything before the blank canvas to the library.

A knot tightened in Sandra's stomach. She entered the car and shut the door. Sandra felt like she was inside a pot of boiling rice. She started the truck and pushed all the power window buttons to lower the windows.

Sandra placed her phone on the magnetic dashboard holder and called Sally. She cranked up the AC, backed out of her spot, and headed toward the library as the phone started ringing, the sound coming through the speakers.

The library was in sight when Sally's voice came over the speakerphone.

"Hello!" said Sally in a squeaky voice. It was followed by a throaty laugh.

Sandra looked up toward the roof of her car, as in giving thanks to the heavens. "Mrs. Paterson?"

"What, Sandra? Did you call me Mrs. Something? Are you okay? It's Sally! Sally!"

Oh my God, thought Sandra, *is she drunk?* Before Sandra could speak, Sally continued.

"We'll talk about that later." Her voice went up two octaves. "Sandra! Where have you been? Oh my God. It was a blast! I sold one of the paintings! Just bring your ass here!" She hung up.

28

Luke

WHEN LUKE BOARDED THE FLIGHT AT LAX, THE TIME WAS 8 a.m. As he rushed through arrivals, zooming past departure gates at Newark liberty, his carryon dragged behind him, an overhead display showed the time as 5:30 p.m. They'd gained a few minutes here and there from some tailwind assist, the pilot had mentioned over the intercom. He wished they'd gained at least an hour, bringing him closer to finding out what had been going on.

He contemplated stopping at a phone booth and calling Sandra or Madden. Then he realized that without his phone, he couldn't access their phone numbers.

"The curse of smartphones," he said to himself. Nobody memorized phone numbers anymore. All he had to do was remember under which name he'd saved a person's number to call them.

Luke was self-conscious as he zipped through fellow travelers, but nobody paid him any attention. Ahead of him, he saw a kiosk with pictures of cell phones and phone accessories.

He slowed down. Maybe he should buy a new charger. It seemed he'd forgotten his, plugged into the wall behind the nightstand at the Hilton. All he had was his earphones.

As Luke got closer to the kiosk, he let out a groan. It was one of those electronic vending kiosks that dispensed small but expensive electronics.

A couple stood in front of it, either purchasing something or window shopping. He slowed, then decided to move on. He would charge his phone in the cab.

Once outside the airport building, the hot and humid summer air hit him like a brick wall—the smell of jet fumes and stale hot dogs from the nearby garbage added to the welcome committee.

Conversations went on in different languages. Cars tooted their horns, and in the background, jet engines roared as they went wheels up.

Luke took off his blazer and stood in line at the kiosk for yellow cabs. When it got to his turn, he gave the confirmation number he'd memorized from the app. They asked for an ID, and he was all set. He was relieved. Getting a cab wasn't as difficult as he'd expected.

"Is this your first time in New Jersey?" asked the cab driver, who could be Indian or Pakistani from his accent.

"No, I grew up here in Beaver Run."

"Ah, nice quiet place. I have family in Parsippany. Not too far from Beaver Run. Yes?"

"Right." Luke saw his opportunity. "Hey, I forgot my charger at the hotel. Is there one I can borrow?"

The driver looked in the rearview mirror. "Of course."

Luke felt like the elephant sitting on his shoulder had finally moved on. "Thank you." He let out a sigh and reached for the cable the driver held up. His hand stopped midair. "You…you don't have an iPhone charger?"

The man shook his head. "No, Samsung. Maybe it's time I bought all the different chargers and kept them in my car."

A good idea, thought Luke, then sank back into the seat. As the car meandered through the evening traffic out of Newark, he wondered how soon he would have to leave Beaver Run for good.

Once he paid Moe and got his car back, he could leave. As soon as tomorrow if he wanted. But the prospect of driving to Los Angeles didn't have him jumping. In fact, the idea of leaving Sandra didn't appeal to him.

The drive was long. The after-work traffic didn't help. But finally, Luke made it to Beaver Run. He got out of the car, not sure how to approach the issue of not tipping.

"Thanks so much," said Luke. He felt so bad he didn't have any cash to tip the guy.

"No, thank you," said the cab driver. "Take care. And thanks for giving me the idea to buy a universal charger for my cab."

A nice guy, Luke thought as the cab driver backed into the road.

Once the car was gone, Luke went to the flowerpot by the entrance. He looked around, and seeing nobody, bent down to retrieve the key.

"Please, please, please," Luke said in a whisper. He raised the pot and reached under. His fingers touched the key, and he let out a sigh of relief.

Luke unlocked the door, and it dawned to him that the Sandra that cared would've taken the key with her so no one would come in. That confirmed the beginning of the end to him.

He opened the door and walked in slowly, tired from the

long flight and then the long drive. He dropped his bag and went to the kitchen to charge his phone.

Luke was eager to find out what happened since he was incommunicado. He hoped the money from Madden was already in his bank account.

To kill time, while waiting for his phone to do a Lazarus since the battery had lost charge completely, he went to the bathroom in the bedroom to pee.

As he washed his hands, he looked at himself in the mirror. Sleepy dull eyes stared back at him. "When is your life finally going to turn around? You get out from one mess and jump into another." He shook his head and sighed. He didn't have the answer.

Luke splashed cold water on his face. The coldness woke him up and tightened his skin. He grabbed the towel hanging by the towel holder, and as he dried his face, he heard the muffled beep of his phone. It had come back to life. He'd been waiting for that.

Luke smiled. "Finally!" Time to find out what had been going on since he'd traveled. He finished with the towel and placed it back.

He walked through the living room and was about to enter the kitchen when he noticed something in his peripheral view.

Luke froze. He took a deep breath and turned.

"No." The area where he'd placed the canvas bag containing his life's work was bare. A chill ran down his spine.

He walked over and looked around. Checked in the bedroom, bathroom even looked under the sofa.

Nothing.

Luke's balls tightened. Like someone had grabbed his scrotum and squeezed.

Sandra was the last person here. Did she move it? He ran

to the kitchen, picked up his phone, unlocked the screen, scrolled once, and tapped Sandra's number.

Luke could not stand still. As it rang, he walked around the house and rechecked all the rooms again. The canvas bag was not there.

Any other person could have easily gotten here, removed the key from under the flowerpot, and taken his life's work. No, stolen his life's work.

Luke couldn't breathe. When the call to Sandra went to voicemail a second time, he thought of calling 911.

His fingers thought for him. He shivered and dialed 911.

"911 operator. What's your emergency?" said a female voice.

"I…I've been robbed."

"What happened?"

"I…I just came back from a trip…my paintings are missing."

"Are you alone?"

"Yes, I've looked around the house."

"Any sign of a break-in?"

"N…no. I left the key under a flowerpot. They must have used it."

"Anybody else know about the location of the key?"

"Yes, the guy I rented the Airbnb from and my…my…" Could Sandra have taken the paintings? To spite him. It wasn't the type of thing she would do. He heard the operator's voice.

"Sir. Sir! Are you still there?"

No wonder she wasn't answering her phone. "Yes, I'm still here."

"What happened?"

"Nothing new. I'm just upset."

"I understand, sir. I'll send an officer your way. He'll be there in five minutes. What's the address?"

Luke hung up. He didn't have five minutes. Since the burglar was no longer here and nobody was hurt, threatened, or in physical danger, they would send local law enforcement. Who knows when they would show up?

The sheriff's office was not far away. Before he knew it, Luke was out of his door running to the sheriff's office. He couldn't believe it. Sandra had stolen his paintings to spite him.

29

Sandra

Earlier that same day at the Beaver Run Library parking lot, Sandra parked under a spot reached by a shadow from the old oak tree.

There were just a few cars in the library, and the coach she was looking for was not one of them. They must have gone back to New York. Something tightened in her stomach.

She got out of the car and tried to slip her phone into her back pocket. But she had on a skirt, so she threw it into her purse.

As Sandra walked up the pavement heading toward the entrance, the municipal bus pulled up beside the curb. Two senior citizens got out.

Sandra would have held the door and waited for them, but she didn't want to keep Bill waiting.

Once inside, her eyes swept the general area looking for Sally. Not seeing her, she went to the section with the art displays.

"Sandra!" It was a hushed yell.

Sandra whirled and saw Sally smiling and waving her over from the children's section.

She walked over, fighting hard to keep in the panic she felt.

Sally threw out her hands, palm up. "Where did you get those people from? They were amazing." Sally paused. "Wait. Did you call me Mrs. Something on the phone? We…" Sally drew her head back, eyebrows narrowed. "What's wrong?"

Sandra exhaled. "Someone is waiting for me at Beaver Tail. Luke sent him." Her voice was flat.

Sally's eyes widened. "Is Luke okay?"

"Yeah, he's fine."

"But…" said Sally. "There's always a big butt somewhere."

Sandra's lips twitched. "The guy's supposed to pick up some paintings and-"

"And it's one of the ones on display here?" asked Sally. "The landscape nude by the lake?"

Something climbed up Sandra's throat, leaving a bitter taste in her mouth. She swallowed hard. "Yes, plus others." Her voice was barely audible.

"I tried to reach you, but Eddie kept on insisting that I sell it to him."

"Eddie?"

"Yes, Eddie. The head of the group. I explained it wasn't mine to sell. And he countered that since I had the authority to exhibit it, I could entertain offers too. I disagreed. But just before they left, he came back with a written agreement."

Sandra was shaking her head. "A written agreement?"

"Yes! He typed it out at the computer station." Sally gestured toward the bank of computers lined up against the wall on her left. "That he was putting fifty percent down payment for the painting and taking possession. And if the artist rejects his offer, he will return the painting."

Sandra shut her eyes, hoping that Sally would tell her she was joking when she opened them. "Oh God, Sally. But there was no price on it. It's part of a batch of ten paintings some guy, Bill Madden, commissioned with Luke. He's here to pick them up."

"Gosh. I feel terrible. All ten are here?"

"No, one is in the municipal building, and the others are here. The rest of his paintings are in the truck. I grabbed the whole bag when I was hurrying to get to you."

"Come," said Sally and walked toward the art display. She stopped at a landscape of a beach. "This was another piece the guy was excited about. Maybe the guy doesn't even know what the paintings look like. You'll just give him this as number ten."

Sandra was already shaking her head. "They had a contract. And a nude was part of it." She let out a shaky breath. "The model Luke had arranged to draw bailed on him, so I...you know. After you gave me the advice. I made him an offer he couldn't refuse. I would be his model if he would…"

Sally's eyes widened. "What?" She lowered her voice conspiratorially. "You slut, get out of Beaver Run."

Sandra would have enjoyed this moment if the situation weren't dire.

Sally giggled. "Wow, sneaky, sneaky. A painting with a salacious story. Oh, I could have gotten more money for the painting after telling that story."

Sandra was devoid of a plan and looked at Sally for a way out.

Sally took a deep breath. As she filled her lungs, she

appeared to step into the character of a responsible mother, grandmother, and librarian. "Do you know how much they agreed on?"

Sandra never liked talking about finance with people, but shit had just become real. "In his text, Luke said I shouldn't hand them over until I logged into a job platform website account he provided. I think both parties have to agree before the funds are released to either of them. The amount he mentioned was a hundred thousand dollars. So I'm assuming ten thousand apiece."

Sally stroked her chin. "Hmmm, that's a lot of money. But an agreement is an agreement. You don't move the post after the kick. Tell you what."

"What?"

"Why don't you go back and talk to this guy, Bill. If it's the nude or nothing, I'll personally drive to New York and collect it from Eddie and bring it back."

Sandra exhaled. People were still looking at the paintings. "I'll take the ones here, pick up the one from the mayor, and present them to Bill."

"Try that. If it doesn't work. I'll drive to Manhattan and bring it back. I think Eddie is an honorable man."

People were still looking at Luke's paintings. It would be rude to just take them. Sandra asked Sally to keep an eye on them.

She went to the mayor's office, told the secretary she needed the painting, and went back to her restaurant.

She broke the news to an impatient but calm Bill Madden.

"I have all the paintings, except the landscape nude. Will you accept another in place of it?"

"Luke and I had an agreement, the nude or nothing," said Bill.

"The painting is in New York. It will be returned in the

next two hours."

Bill closed his eyes and shook his head. When he opened them, there was a glint of humor and happiness in them. He let out a deep breath.

"I was hoping for that. It nullifies the agreement."

Sandra's eyebrows shot up. "What do you mean? I could have gone without informing you and returned two hours later, nobody the wiser."

"But you didn't. Luke's agreement with me was clear. Both parties have to agree for the funds to be released." Bill sighed and leaned back into his chair.

Sandra folded her hands over her chest and glared at him.

"I'm really sorry for you getting involved in this. I'm a businessman, and I do speculative art buying. I'd hoped Luke Martin would have broken out like a penny stock by now and soared with eagles." He shook his head. "It didn't happen. It seems he enjoys scratching the ground with chickens."

Sandra knew what he alluded to but asked anyway. "What do you mean?"

"I'd hoped Luke's work would be well known by now, and I could make a profit from my investment, but still, nobody knows him. He has amazing skills, but his works are not known."

Sandra understood. It was the same reason she'd put Luke's work out there.

Bill continued. "My funds are tied up in escrow, and I need them now. We had a clause in the contract we drew. Unfortunately, not delivering on time was one of the stipulations we agreed on that could nullify the contract. I'll have to take my leave now. Thanks so much for the meal." He started to get up.

"But…but-"

"Don't worry," said Bill. "Look at it from a more positive

way. It went well. We agreed to disagree."

Sandra sat there and watched him head to the exit. How the fuck did she get mixed up in this crap? The way things were now, the least she could do was get back the painting. But the more she thought about it, the more it was clear it was her fault.

If she'd just left things the way they were, left Luke to his own devices as he'd left her four years ago, she wouldn't be in this mess. At the end of the day, it was her fault. She'd just yanked food out of Luke's mouth-a hundred thousand dollars' worth.

A shaky breath rattled out of Sandra. She headed for the door, oblivious of other people in the restaurant.

"Everything okay?" asked the hostess as she passed.

"Yeah." She didn't look at her. "I'll be at the library."

Back at the library, Sandra found Sally by the exhibition.

The exhibition had wound down with a few stragglers admiring the paintings. Sally stood with a folder in her hand with an older couple looking at oil on canvas of a bridge Sandra thought was the Golden Gate Bridge in San Francisco.

"You said a local artist painted this?" asked the old man in a hoarse voice.

"Born and bred," said Sally.

"But there's nothing local about it," said the woman with the man. Her voice was soft, barely audible.

Sally looked up and saw Sandra watching. "Excuse me," she said to the couple and walked toward Sandra.

Sandra tried to smile and look positive, but her smile fluttered.

"I guess it didn't go well," said Sally.

"Nope. He didn't even give it a chance. He just wanted out of the contract to release his tied-up funds. He said Luke was scratching the ground for food like chickens."

Sally made a face. "He said that?"

"Well, something like that."

"Loser!" said Sally into open space and stuck out her tongue.

Self-conscious as if Sally had referred to her, Sandra glanced around, met a few people's eyes, then smoothed her clothes. "I guess it's New York then."

"You didn't ask me how much Eddie wanted the painting for," said Sally as she walked toward a window overlooking the parking lot.

Sandra followed. Outside the window, the white town bus dropped off another batch of people in the parking lot. "It kept skipping my mind. Eddie is a retiree. Paintings are things rich-"

Sally had a smile on her face like someone had proposed to perform an act she enjoyed on her. She opened the folder she was holding and brought out a piece of paper. "Here."

Sandra took it and started to read. It was the agreement Eddie had written up. Her hands began to shake, rattling the paper. Sandra held it with both hands. She couldn't believe her eyes. "He…" She cleared her throat and swallowed. "He agreed to pay two hundred thousand dollars for one painting?"

Sally nodded and smiled. She handed Sandra another piece of paper.

It was a check made out to Luke Martin for one hundred thousand dollars. Sandra's heartbeat fluttered in her chest like the wings of a canary caught in a hunter's net. "Oh my God. Oh my God. I have to call Luke." She looked around, confused. "Where's my phone? It's in my handbag…in the car. I hope he has landed." She gave the paper and the check back to Sally. "I don't know what to say. I'll be right back."

30

Luke

LUKE STOPPED RUNNING AND WALKED ONCE HE CAUGHT SIGHT of the station. He inhaled through his nose and exhaled through his mouth, trying to catch his breath.

He'd sprinted most of the way. Sweat trickled down his forehead, down his face to his chest, soaking his T-shirt. His lungs burned.

Luke turned to the sound of a powerful engine. A white bus with *Beaver Run Transport* written on the side drove past him. He watched it turn into the street he was headed to, drive past the sheriff's office, and continue toward the library.

On a typical day, Luke would have gone the same way on the pavement as the bus. But the shortest distance between two points is a straight line. He cut across the lawn—something he rarely did.

He knew the layout of the station from when he'd visited with Stone barely two weeks ago. It felt like it was months ago. He climbed up the stairs, and for the first time, doubt crept into his mind.

Were his emotions driving him? Was he really going to go in there and tell them that he thought Sandra stole his paintings?

Luke thought of all the canvases he'd painted over the years. The sweat and tears he'd poured into each one of them, and now they were gone. It was difficult to comprehend. The feeling left a deep hollow in his chest.

He slammed that emotional door shut and ran up the stairs to the sheriff's office.

Luke pulled open the glass door and stepped in, feeling like he'd stepped into a freezer. A big painted text in front of him said *Welcome to Beaver Run Sheriff's Office.*

A cushioned wooden bench was pushed against the wall. The air-conditioner came alive right at that moment, blowing cool air with a faint smell of bleach. Soaked with sweat, goosebumps spread all over Luke's skin.

Someone to his left cleared their throat, and Luke turned.

A young man, twenty-three or twenty-four, stood behind the counter, dressed in the green-colored uniform of a sheriff's deputy. Behind him was what looked like a general office with desks and computers. Luke could hear voices but couldn't see who was talking.

"Can I help you, sir?"

Luke walked over to the deputy, not sure what to say. It would be ludicrous to just turn around and walk away. He was already here. He decided to press on. But the way the man looked at him... His appearance-he must look like an overused dab-it foam.

Luke placed his palms on the counter looked down at himself, then at the officer. "Sorry, I ran all the way once I discovered I'd been robbed."

The deputy's eyes flickered, but he tried to keep his features calm. "You were robbed? Where?"

"At the Airbnb I'm renting. I came back after a trip to California and found that all my paintings were gone."

"Was there forced entry? What's your address?"

Luke shook his head slowly. "No." He lowered his eye, then returned them to look at the deputy. "Ummm, I left the key under a flowerpot. Moronic, right?"

The deputy brought a pen and paper. "What's your address again?"

The deputy repeated back Luke's words as he wrote. "29 Winery…" His head shot up. "That's Deputy Stone's address." He pointed at Luke. "Wait, you're the artist Trevor's sister is hanging out with. I mean Deputy Leigh."

Heat rushed to Luke's cheeks. "She stole my paintings! She's the only one that knew I was gone and where the key was!"

The deputy blinked rapidly as if trying to comprehend what he'd just heard. *"What…"* He glanced back at the office layout behind him and raised a finger. "Wait please, one second." He walked back to the office area.

Luke was ashamed of his outburst. But why did the deputy walk away? He shouldn't have come here. He'd acted too hastily. He should have waited to at least hear from Sandra.

What about Madden? He could easily do something like that. Luke brought out his phone and tapped on the text message icon. He tapped on Madden's text and scrolled down and read the message from Madden. He'd sent his address to Madden.

Like some type of *juju,* a text came in from Madden right at that moment. Luke tapped on it and read quickly. *Sorry buddy. Your girlfriend blew it. Contract nullified. Paintings incomplete.*

Incomplete? All the paintings were there when he left. His text to Sandra was clear on what to do. Did she give Bill all the pieces? Luke's pounding heartbeat sounded like supersonic booms in his head and ears.

A missed call notification from Sandra appeared on his phone. A thousand thoughts ran through his mind.

"Luke! What is this I hear?" said a familiar voice.

Luke looked up. Trevor Leigh approached from the opposite side of the counter. He was the last person Luke wanted to see. He'd just accused his sister of robbing him.

"Hi, Trevor."

Trevor chuckled. He nodded toward the deputy. "James here said you think Sandra"—he made quotation marks in the air—"stole your paintings?" He shook his head. "You two lovebirds. Your paintings are on exhibition at the library. You didn't know?"

"What...I just came back from California."

"Ah," said Trevor. "She must have wanted to surprise you." He laughed and shook his head.

"S...surprise me?"

"Yeah. Your paintings are on exhibition at the library as we speak. I haven't gone yet, but people that have are raving about your work. I think Sandra is there right now. I saw her car as I-"

Luke was already heading toward the door. He raised his hand to wave at Trevor. It all made sense now. The fucking exhibition. He took the stairs two at a time. He hit the ground and dashed off toward the library.

Luke rushed into the library and stopped in front of the reception area to collect his thoughts.

The library looked so small from the last time he visited, probably when he was in high school.

He glanced around, noticing the differences since the last time he was there. A 3D printer station. A bank of Mac computers against the wall, a silent room, and new furniture.

He saw the sign for the art exhibit and headed in that direction. He barely noticed the other people in the library.

Luke felt like a knife had been plunged into his heart with each painting he saw on display. They were for him and him alone. How dare Sandra put them up for everyone to see and judge?

He saw one of his older works he hadn't looked at in years. Luke would have patted himself on the back if he wasn't so tense. Then he saw Sandra coming toward him, smiling.

"Luke! You're back. I've been trying to reach you." She spread out her arms wide for a hug.

Despite his anger, her smile disarmed him. His frozen heart thawed just a little bit. Grudgingly he hugged her back.

She tapped his shoulders and squeezed. "You're sweaty and wound tight like a mountain lion about to spring. Relax." She massaged his shoulder.

Luke hissed. "You've got that right. I just got a text from Madden. What happened? He said the contract was canceled. You didn't deliver. I was looking forward to that money." His eyes darted from one display of his work to another. "And who gave you permission to display my work?"

He felt her stiffen beside him.

He knew he'd crossed a line, but he couldn't help himself.

Sandra spoke through clenched teeth. "Mrs. Paterson told me about the exhibit, and I said *Why not?*"

"She told me too, and I said no," said Luke, his voice rising. "Didn't we talk about it before I left?"

"Yes, we did and-"

A voice had shushed them.

They both paused and looked around.

"Come," said Sandra and headed toward the exit. "Let's take this outside."

Luke followed, suddenly developing a facial twitch.

"Sandra!"

They both turned.

It was Mrs. Paterson. She walked toward them at a brisk pace. "Hi, Luke."

Luke's lips went through the motion of a smile. "Hello."

Mrs. Paterson leaned close to Sandra and whispered something in her ear. Sandra nodded.

Sally handed her a folder. "See you guys." She turned and walked away.

Outside in the parking lot, the argument started small. Sandra pleaded with him, her tone reconciliatory.

"Luke, everyone that saw your paintings commented on how talented you are. You are a talented artist. Your work has to be made available for people to see. That's why I brought them out here. What are you afraid of?"

"I'm not afraid of anything. My paintings are for me. The ones for other people are the ones they commissioned me to do. Where are the rest? They're not here on display and not in the house."

"Oh." Sandra gestured to her truck with her thumb. "In there. I was in a hurry and grabbed the whole bag."

"Shit…I thought I was robbed. I even went to the sheriff's office to report."

"Really? You thought I stole your paintings?"

Luke sidestepped the question. "What happened with Madden?"

Sandra sighed. "I saw your bank account ATM receipt. I heard Moe on the answering machine…I was only trying to help. You would not take money from me."

"Of course, I wouldn't. I'm not a gigolo."

Sandra laughed. "Man-whore fits you better." She sighed. "Luke, I was only trying to help…I didn't know you had an arrangement with Madden."

"What happened with him?" Luke asked again.

Sandra let out a breath. "Okay, to cut a long story short, someone bought the landscape nude while it was exhibited. I told Bill to give me two hours to get it back, but he refused. Said something about it was a basis to void the contract."

Luke ran his fingers through his hair. "My God, Sandra! Yes, money is tight, but I knew it was coming. I just lined up more work in California."

"I'm so sorry. I didn't mean to cause you any problems."

Luke sighed. "Of course, you didn't." He took a deep breath and let it out slowly through his nose. His shoulders dragged down with the exhale.

He shook his head, then fixed his gaze at her. "Things never change," said Luke slowly. "It's always Luke do this… do that…don't do that. You're always trying to get me to do things I don't want to do. I don't do exhibitions!"

Startled, Sandra took a step back.

The fight suddenly left Luke. He raised a finger and drew a circle in the air. When he spoke next, his voice was low. "Things have come full circle just like four years ago…if only you would mind your business."

As soon as the word left Luke's mouth, he knew he'd just dropped an egg. The initial look on Sandra's face at that moment was like a prologue to a tsunami.

The surprise as the waves receded. The fear, then anger,

as you realize you'd wasted precious escape time marveling at the phenomena as the killer waves rushed back toward you with a vengeance.

Luke knew that whatever this woman felt for him, a flickering light had just been extinguished by him.

31

Sandra

SANDRA WATCHED HIM. HER WHOLE BODY SHOOK IN SYNC TO the whoosh, whoosh, whoosh sound inside her head and the pounding of her heart.

Breathe. Breathe.

Sandra did precisely that.

He'd hurt her before. Blamed her for his own inadequacies-he'd done it again just like that. She *must* hurt him back.

Luke squirmed under her gaze. His lips moved, but no words came out.

Sandra remembered Sally's words to her minutes ago. *Don't throw the kitchen sink at him. Leave some things unsaid, so there can be room to make up.* Right now, she was going to drop the house on him.

"It...it didn't come out right," said Luke.

"You know," said Sandra, "I can't deal with this anymore. It took a while, but I weaned myself off you. Not that I had a choice. You were already gone. I don't know why you decided to come back to Beaver Run and paint. There are so many other small towns you could have gone to." She exhaled. "Yes, go. Go to California and find another Bill Madden and get paid peanuts for your work. What is the use of creating art if you can't share your talent with the world? I'll drop off the paintings at your place."

Luke looked like he was going to say something, at least apologize. He stared at her.

Her heart breaking, but still expecting to hear the magic words, Sandra gazed at him, her chest rising and falling. But the words didn't come. She waved a palm in finality at him. "Forget it."

Sandra turned and walked toward her vehicle. She opened the door and was about to get in when she realized the folder was still in her hand. She walked back to him.

Luke straightened himself, chest puffed out with a smug look on his face. Like she'd finally come to her senses and would get on her knees and beg him.

Sandra was going to wipe that look off his face. She pushed the folder toward him.

Luke's eyebrows narrowed. He reached for it. "What is it?"

"You're right, Luke. Nothing has changed. Always taking the easy way out. I thought I loved you, that you were special. But after you breezed into town, I realized it was only the sex I'd missed. I've gotten my fill, and honestly, Peter is even better."

Sandra hadn't as much as held hands with Peter, but she got the desired response as she gazed at Luke.

He looked like a worm exhausted from wriggling furiously after having been doused with salt.

32

Luke

LUKE HAD AN OUT-OF-BODY EXPERIENCE. LIKE HE WAS above, watching himself watching Sandra.

She climbed into her truck, shut the door, and for a moment stared ahead. Then she sighed, pulled down the seatbelt, strapped herself in, and reached for the ignition.

The roar as Sandra's powerful engine came to life jarred him out of the fugue state he was in.

His eyes trailed her truck all the way to the road until it was out of sight, and the deep rumble of her engine faded to oblivion.

A loud silence engulfed Luke like a winter coat, devoid of warmth and comfort. Having driven away the only person that had always been there for him, he was all alone and out of money.

He looked around to see if anyone else had witnessed the drama that had just unfolded in the parking lot. Movement in a library window caught his eye. Someone had ducked out of view as he looked. He was sure it was Mrs. Paterson. Well, there was nothing else to see. The party was over.

Luke couldn't just stand in the middle of the library parking lot sweaty, smelly, and tired. He added broke to that list. He might as well head home.

Shoulders slumped, he walked toward the road. The only option he had now money-wise was to accept Baltimore's offer.

He reached for his phone in his back pocket then stopped. He'd made a lot of hasty decisions. California was definitely in his future, but let him sleep on it.

Luke wondered where Sandra had taken off to. Maybe she went back to her restaurant. No. Too emotional right now to talk to other people.

Cars zipped past him on the road, and he wondered what the people inside those cars were thinking about. Were they happy, sad, or both? He wondered what people thought as they watched him pounding the pavement.

Apart from Mrs. Paterson, who he was sure had watched the debacle unfold in the parking lot, Luke assumed that each time he was in public, someone was watching him. But each time he looked around, nobody was.

But this time, he was wrong. Someone was indeed watching him.

"Luke!"

Luke halted, and his head swung in the direction the voice came from.

Moe's garage. Wow, he'd walked that far already?

Moe stood in front of his garage in a dirty navy blue overall with a scowl on his face. Behind him was the open garage with a car suspended about four feet high. Moe looked tired but alert. He waved Luke over.

Luke was thankful for the interruption but apprehensive.

Unbreak Her heart

He didn't have the money to pay for his car yet. He saw his car parked to the side and wondered how Moe would respond when he told him he didn't have the money.

"You look like you carry all the problems of Beaver Run on your shoulders!"

Luke barely heard him above the whine and stutter of an air wrench and the continuous buzz of an industrial fan close to the garage exit.

"It's a long walk to the library!" said Luke. "I'm on my way home now."

Moe walked away from the garage toward Luke's car. "I called and left you a couple of messages. Your car has been ready for some time."

"Sorry, I was in LA, just came in a few hours ago."

"Ah, now I see why the long face. You miss California already? Beaver Run can do that to you."

Luke laughed. He hadn't expected any humor from him, but so right he was. Beaver Run had fucked him up.

Moe pointed to Luke's car. "We need the space. You have a new battery, a new alternator, spark plugs, and we changed the oil. As good as new-now get it out of here. The key is in the ignition."

Luke looked at Moe again, surprised. He had never heard him say so much in one breath.

Moe pointed at the garage entrance. "One of the boys saw your work at the library. Now he wants to pick up doodling at his spare time." He shook his head. "He doesn't understand every person has their own calling."

Luke smiled. "You never know. There might be a Caravaggio hiding inside him."

"Michelangelo Caravaggio? Yeah right."

Luke's eyebrows shot up. "You know his work?"

Moe smiled. "To me, he was the best. He drew what he

saw. You have a mole growing out of your nose. He drew it in. No 17th century Photoshopping."

Luke threw his head back and laughed. For a moment, he forgot his many predicaments. "Which one is your favorite?"

"Ah, that's easy. The Seven Works of Mercy."

Luke nodded. "An interesting piece." He folded his hands over his chest.

It was created in 1607 by the Baroque master and depicted the seven corporal works of mercy. To feed the hungry, give drink to the thirsty, clothe the naked, give travelers shelter, visit the sick, the imprisoned, and bury the dead.

Caravaggio had expertly depicted more than half of the seven mercies in his painting with the image of a woman breastfeeding her starving father in prison.

Moe wagged a finger at Luke, then paused as if he were contemplating something. He had that embarrassed look people have when they have a confession to make.

"You remind me of your mother," said Moe.

Luke froze. For a few seconds, he just stared at him. "You knew my mother?"

33

Luke

MOE NODDED. "SHE WAS A FIRST-CLASS ARTIST. I KNEW YOUR father too."

The day was becoming too much for Luke. "But I never met you. You never visited."

"I lived in Rockaway then. We've met before, but you were a baby then. Your dad always came to Rockaway to visit until his health got awfully bad. I used to visit him at the hospice."

"Maurice…Moe." Luke nodded. He remembered seeing the visitors' log at the hospice with the name Maurice M.

"I was surprised and happy when Sandra brought you."

"How did you know my father?"

"We worked together at the plastic factory in Newton before I decided to become an auto mechanic full-time. Cars had been a passion of mine."

Moe went on and on, and Luke tried to remain patient. He wanted to know more about his parents, not about Moe. At a point, he knew that if he didn't say anything, Moe might talk all night. "So you and my father worked in Newton."

"Yes. Like I said, my passion was cars, your father's...his was your mother."

Moe paused as if to collect his thoughts. "Your father was always a man of very few words, and so was your mother. She worked as a secretary in the office where we worked, and Dave loved her from afar. He would come into the office, clock in, say hi to her, and then leave. At the end of his shift, he would come in, clock out, and say bye." Moe inhaled and then let it out in a rush.

Luke stood there transfixed. He'd never heard anything like that about his parents before.

Moe continued. "This went on for two years, and I knew that if I didn't intervene, nothing would happen."

"What did you do?" asked Luke, amused that his parents were plagued with the same problem as most young people.

"So I tricked them," said Moe. "I told Nancy that Dave wanted to take her out. It turned out she had also loved him from afar. They got together, things worked out fine, and they got married. Your father loved everything about Nancy and worshiped the ground she walked on. They had a few years of happiness, then they got pregnant. That was the happiest day of your father's life."

"Really?" That had always bothered me. "I thought he never wanted children." Growing up, I felt my father hated me. Granted, he made sure I had a roof over my head, clothes, and food-but that was it. I was just lucky. I didn't run with the wrong crowds and found joy creating art.

"Why didn't he want me?"

"No, he did. That was before they got the news."

Luke's eyes widened. "What news?

"Your mother was diagnosed with some sort of aggressive

cancer."

"But I thought she died from complications from giving birth to me."

Moe shook his head. "No...no."

Luke felt a tingling in his chest. Like he was on a roller coaster at Six Flags, and they'd just reached the top of the track. The cars were going to drop, and that sickening feeling was coming. He couldn't just get out of the ride. He braced himself.

Moe had been talking.

"Sorry, you said she refused what?"

"The cancer treatment would harm the developing fetus, so your mother refused it."

Luke felt like the ride had dropped, pushing his stomach into his throat. "Oh my God."

"Your father didn't hate you. He just hated what you reminded him of."

"Isn't that the same thing?" said Luke. "Hate is hate."

"Let me finish. To your father, your mother loved you more."

"But I'm half him, half her."

"Yes, but you were a stranger to him. Your mother was his joy." Moe exhaled. "He didn't understand the bond of motherhood. Most men don't get it."

Luke now knew the position his father had been in.

"All right, kid. I have to go."

Luke touched his pocket and was about to say he didn't have his wallet with him when Moe spoke.

"I've already turned the computer off. Come back whenever, and we can take care of that. In the meantime, keep on painting."

Moe turned and headed toward the garage.

Luke watched him go. "Thank you." It occurred to him

he'd been doing a lot of that today, watching people walk away.

Moe spun around and walked back. "You know, by the lake, close to the abandoned drawstring bridge, beavers have completely taken over. Capturing the beavers at work creating dams, doing the things that gave this town its name would look good on canvas."

"I'll check it out."

"Just a thought. My regards to Ms. Sandra."

The mention of Sandra brought him back to his predicament. Luke lowered himself onto the car's worn leather seat. He ran his palms over the steering wheel. He took a deep breath, inhaling the smell of old leather and gasoline—the latter probably from the mechanics.

He started the car, closed his eyes, and leaned his head against the headrest, enjoying the purr of the engine. It felt like home. He'd missed his car.

Luke engaged the gear and drove out. The engine and drive were smooth. Instead of driving to the Airbnb, Luke found himself on the road to his father's house. The house where he grew up.

The sky was darker as he drove past the three-bedroom, two-and-a-half-bath ranch. The lights were on. Someone was home and moved around in the living room. Should he stop and tell them he used to live there? No, they might say make an appointment or just call the cops.

Luke continued driving. He remembered his father, and the fact they rarely spoke even though they lived in the same house was the only memory that came to mind. Moe's insight had really helped him see his dad's motivations.

Luke remembered the old duffel bag he'd collected from storage. Maybe now was a good time to look at it. Luke turned around and headed to his place.

34

Sandra

SANDRA WAS ON HER WAY TO THE RESTAURANT UNTIL SHE looked in the rearview mirror and noticed tears on her face. She wiped them with the back of her hand. She wasn't going to let anyone see her like that and start asking questions.

She also caught sight of the canvas bag with the paintings. She would drop them off at Luke's place now she was sure he wasn't home.

Sandra couldn't understand why trying to help someone you cared for became 'not minding your business.' They had history. Was she trying to fit a circle in a square hole?

The thought jarred her. Maybe it was not meant to be. She should just settle with Peter, but she wasn't feeling him at all.

Why was she even crying for someone that didn't love her?

Sandra turned into the street that led to his house. She would open the door, drop off the paintings, and be gone.

The motion lights came on as she approached. Sandra lifted the gargoyle flowerpot-there was no key.

Of course, he took the key after thinking she'd stolen his work. Beaver Run was safe. Her brother was in law enforcement, and she knew more than the average inhabitants.

She wasn't going to come back here again. If the paintings got stolen after she left them there, that was Luke's chance at a real problem instead of a made-up one.

Sandra placed the bag with the artwork against the door, thought of leaving a note, then shook her head. "Nope, it's over."

She drove toward her home in her car and tuned the radio to a random station. It was a talk show, and of course, the topic was politics. It was better than any love ballad right now.

Sandra pulled into her driveway a few minutes later. She didn't open the garage, just sat in the car.

She kept on asking herself, *What next, what next?* The talk show was just background noise.

Then her phone started to ring. Heart pounding, Sandra fished it out of her purse and looked at the screen. She was disappointed. It was a number she didn't recognize. Probably a telemarketer.

Sandra was in the right frame of mind to waste the marketer's time and give them a dose of their medicine. She tapped her screen to answer it.

"Hello."

"Hello, Sandra? It's me, Alexis!"

"What...Alex! How are you? I thought you'd forgotten about us."

"No, how can I forget my big sister?"

"Where are you?"

"I'm in the city of love!"

Unbreak Her heart

"Where…what is the city of love?"

"Paris, of course! I'm hanging out with friends, and I thought about you. I'm having a blast. I spoke with Mom, and she said you're seeing Luke Martin again."

"Ummm…well-"

"I thought he was a bastard after what he did to you in college."

He's still a bastard, thought Sandra.

"But being in the city of love makes me think of all the possibilities. Anyway, I gotta go. Kiss, kiss, kiss!"

"Hello?" All Sandra heard was the disengaged tone. She'd hung up.

Sandra shook her head. "The city of love." For the next few minutes, every now and then, she muttered *The city of love*.

Alexis had really made her evening. She never told her she thought Luke was a bastard, which to her credit, was on point. Maybe she'd consumed a lot of wine in the city of love too, and that was the wine talking.

Sandra caught sight of her smiling face in the mirror, and the happiness faded.

She put her car in reverse and backed out of her driveway.

She put the car in drive and took off. Sandra hadn't planned it, but soon she found herself in her parents' driveway. The home where she grew up.

Seeing her mother's car in the driveway, she rang the bell instead of using her key.

"Hi, I wasn't expecting you," said her mother as she stepped out of the way. "Busy day? You're in a suit, and it's late."

"Hi, Mom." Sandra stepped in and closed the door. "I was in the neighborhood and decided to stop by."

"You were in the neighborhood?" Her mother paused.

"Okay, come and tell me all about it. I was just about to make coffee."

Sandra followed her mom to the kitchen. "What about Dad?".

Her mother opened a cabinet and brought out a mug. "He's upstairs, he'll come down once he smells coffee."

Soon both Sandra and her mother sat on bar stools in the kitchen island with steaming mugs of coffee in front of them.

Her mother took a sip and nodded her head. "This is good."

Sandra took a sip. "Definitely good coffee."

Her mother let out a breath and let it out. "Okay, I don't want to spend the next hour sipping coffee and nodding my head. Let's get straight to the grizzly in the room."

Sandra was sure Sally had called her mom. "Okay, what do you want to talk about?"

Her mother drew back. "What do *I* want to talk about?" She exhaled, straightened up, and made a stop sign with both hands. "Okay, I heard from the grapevine that the exhibition went well. I also heard there was an argument in the parking lot of the venue, and the people involved weren't singing hosanna."

Sandra looked like she was going to break down. "Mom…I gave him another chance, and he's doing the same thing he did four years ago."

Sandra's mother covered her hand with hers. "I know, I know. Sometimes it takes a crooked path to get to love. And sometimes we don't even recognize it when it hits us on the head." Her mother paused. "Does he love you?"

"No," said Sandra quickly. After a few seconds. "I think so. But he's hung up on something. I don't know anymore. I'm tired."

"You love him, obviously. You've always loved him. I

remember when you suddenly became interested in art in high school."

"You knew?" said Sandra feeling heat rush to her cheeks.

"Of course. Mothers know their children better than their children know themselves."

She nodded.

"You know about his mother, right?"

"Of course. She died giving birth to him. Everybody knows that."

"No, she was diagnosed with cancer, and she opted not to treat because of the potential of the treatment being harmful to the unborn baby. She was pregnant with Luke when she was diagnosed. His father wanted her to get rid of the pregnancy, but she refused."

Sandra covered her mouth with her hands. "I never heard that before."

"Well, that's grown-up territory. By the time Luke was born, it was too late. The cancer was aggressive. I think Dave, Luke's father, never forgave him. You don't have to physically hit someone to abuse them. I think his father blaming him for his loss made him withhold his love from Luke." Sandra's mother shrugged. "That's my two cents. I've had time to think about it over the years. What would I have done if I were in Nancy's shoes?"

Nobody said anything. The question just hung in the air.

Sandra's mom continued. "You guys keep on circling back to each other, so I think there might be something there."

"Hey, I smell coffee!" her father shouted from the top of the stairs. "I'm on my way."

It was followed by the sound of footsteps coming down the stairs.

"How do you want your coffee?" asked her mother as soon as her dad walked into the kitchen.

Dad looked at her for a second. "Surprise me."

"Hi, Dad," said Sandra.

"Sandra, guess what? I was at the library today, and what did I see? Paintings from Luke. You know my sister Margaret, your Aunt Marge, God bless her memory. She was married to an artist. Worked herself to death trying to support the family. I don't think he ever sold any paintings."

Sandra's heart sank. It was one thing to have problems with Luke. Still, another having to deal with validation from your dad about why hanging onto a sinking ship wasn't a good idea. Especially when you have options.

"But today," continued her father, "I saw Luke's work, and while I was there, some dude wrote a check. Impressive!"

That must have been Mr. Murphy, thought Sandra.

Mom handed him a mug of coffee. "Here."

Dad blew at the surface, then took a sip. "Hmmm the best. Woman, you'll marry yourself a good husband."

Mom smiled. "Foolishness."

Dad continued. "My concern with painters and writers is them being able to live off of their art. Art is subjective, and no matter how great one person thinks their work is, someone else thinks it's garbage. What I saw at the library was promising. He *REALLY* could make a living selling his works."

Sandra felt a touch of pride but killed it right away. She was no longer rooting for team Luke.

"So…" Dad cleared his throat. "You could…see how it goes with Luke. Just keep Peter as a backup, in case…"

"Backup?" asked Sandra.

"You know, like a spare tire, donut, in case something goes wrong."

Her mother stared at her father. "Spare? In case what?"

"Okay," said her father. "I think I've said a lot and gone off-script. I'll take my coffee in the living room."

After her dad was out of earshot, her mom spoke. "Where was I? He could be lost too, looking for the proverbial light at the end of the tunnel. Sandra, you've always been his light. It might be a situation where you're like the lighthouse in the middle of a storm guiding a ship."

Sandra nodded. Still not sure what to do.

"Come on. Let's go watch some TV."

They moved to the living room and joined Dad watching Family Feud.

After an episode, her dad cocked his head and said, "That sounds like rain."

Sandra looked out of the window and saw it coming down in sheets, pelting the window.

"You might as well spend the night here," said her mother. "There's no need exposing yourself to dangerous driving in this weather."

A few hours later, Sandra lay on her bed in her old room. The clatter of rain against her window and the flash of lightning brought back nostalgic feelings of her teenage years, and Luke was a part of it.

She knew what her mother said about her being Luke's shining light was true and had legs, but could it walk? She couldn't just wait around for him to come around. She didn't have that kind of time.

It takes two to tango, they say. The more she thought about Luke, the more her heart felt like a seesaw in the playground. Up with love one moment and down with the pain of abandonment the next.

35

Luke

THE FIRST THING HE SAW ONCE HE PULLED IN WAS THE canvas bag containing the paintings. It reminded him how foolish he must have looked when he thought Sandra had stolen from him.

The fact that Sandra dropped them there spoke volumes. Beaver Run was safe.

He removed the key from his pocket and unlocked the door. Leaving it open, he brought in the canvas bag and locked the door.

Luke went into the bathroom in his bedroom and took a desperately needed shower. He dried himself and put on his checkered lounge pants and a T-shirt from his closet.

He grabbed the duffel bag they'd picked up from storage and went back to the living room.

He opened it. Inside the bag were some old magazines: *Playboy, Penthouse, Hustler, National Geographic*. His father must have saved them for some reason. He flipped through in case he'd stored some receipts or important documents in them.

Luke perused some of the articles in the girly magazines. He was surprised most of the pieces were not about sex as he'd expected, but short stories and serious non-fiction written by some big names today.

Luke set them aside for later and focused on a Ziplock bag with a worn moleskin diary.

He opened it and saw his father's familiar scrawl on a journal. He'd found his father's journal.

Luke started to read. It was like confirmation from the grave. His father blamed him for his wife's death, just as Moe had said. But his father went further, writing how difficult it was to look at his son.

The boy was a constant reminder of the love he'd lost and who was responsible for that loss. When it came time for the love of his life to choose, she chose their unborn child.

On many occasions, his father wrote, *She chose the baby and not me. She pretended she loved me.*

Luke tried to see things his father's way. Not that his father hated him; he was incapable. He was handicapped by his loss to show him love. In one line he wrote, *I would gladly swap his life for yours, but it wouldn't bring you back.*

As a child, Luke had craved his father's love and affection. His father would be nice one day and hate him the next.

Luke constantly felt his father was mad with him but couldn't figure out what he had done that pissed him off.

As Luke got older, he believed that people's love was temporary. They would cease to love him once they got to know him. To forestall that, he would push them away. The way to accomplish that was to pack and leave abruptly.

Luke sat up straight as the realization hit him.

He hadn't moved away because he was looking for

money or opportunity. That was the excuse, the lie his mind fed him. No, he was pushing people that loved him away first so that they won't fall out of love with him.

Luke now understood his father's love for his mother. The other side of that coin was hatred. A blinding affection his father took too far. Now Luke was doing the same thing. Trying to avoid pain by pushing people away before they stopped loving him.

Everything Sandra did for him was out of love, not meddling.

He remembered what Laura said that first day he'd arrived in Beaver Run. It was only weeks ago, but it felt like a lifetime. Stone accepted the reality he was in love with Adela and moved in with her. That was what real men did.

When Laura said it, it had meant nothing to him, but now he knew better.

He had wronged Sandra, and this time he'd broken the camel's back. He had to find her before it was too late. Before she got any more serious with Peter. He wouldn't be like his father anymore. He was going to be a real man.

Luke remembered the file Sandra had given him. What was in it? To make amends, he had to start somewhere. It was in his car. He slipped on his sneakers and opened the door.

The air was heavy with the smell of rain—the sounds of crickets replaced by the rustling of leaves as trees swayed in the wind.

He dashed to the car, opened the door, and the familiar odor hit him again. It was comforting, like saying to him that everything would be all right.

He grabbed the file and ran for the house, the first drops of rain pelting him like a hundred Nerf gun bullets.

Luke kicked off his sneakers, went to the kitchen, and

yanked out a few sheets of paper towel from the roll. He wiped his hands and face, then dabbed the file.

He walked back to the living room, opened the folder, took out the contents, and dropped the file on the table.

He looked at the agreement first. "What's this?" Luke read it.

I, Edward Murphy of dash dash dash York City hereby deposit fifty percent down payment for the painting, Landscape Nude, by Luke Martin, and take possession. To bring the balance in three days, the 18th of July. If the artist, Luke Martin, rejects this offer, I will return the painting in exchange for the check.

Edward Murphy had signed and dated the document.

Luke put the agreement aside and flipped the check over. "What the f-"

Luke stared at the check, not believing his eyes. "Holy smokes."

He collapsed on the couch, and his hands started to tremble. He remembered one time in second grade when every kid had been picked up after school, and his father was late. A fourth-grade teacher on after-school duty had asked him if she could call his mother instead to come and get him.

Luke had tried to keep a brave face. He knew his mother was never going to come and believed his father had finally abandoned him.

He'd jutted out his lips. His cheeks twitched, his lips quivered, then the tears started to flow. He couldn't stop it then, and he couldn't stop it now.

Luke didn't know how long he cried for the hurt he'd caused Sandra, but he knew he had a problem: how to convince her that his change of heart came before seeing the check.

He would find a way. He must make it right.

36

Sandra

SANDRA DIDN'T FALL ASLEEP UNTIL THE EARLY HOURS OF THE morning. She always woke up with the first light like an early bird hoping to surprise a worm. She would have given an arm to sleep a few more hours.

Daylight streaked into her bedroom through gaps in her curtain, and she knew that falling back to sleep was now an illusion.

Sandra's head throbbed like she had been awake all night drinking. She checked the time on her phone and groaned. Altogether, she'd gotten only about two hours of sleep.

The events of yesterday at the library played through her mind and didn't help her headache. It was just one piece of bad news after the other. Luke relocating to LA. The contract for the paintings falling through and him saying she had to take her nose out of other people's business. It hurt considering all her actions had been for his betterment because she loved him.

Even though she'd gone in with the intentions of just having fun, she'd been swept off her feet and had fallen in love with him—again.

Sandra went to the bathroom, peed, brushed her teeth, and washed her face. She must get on with her routine for the day, and not let this bad experience derail the rest of her week. She made her bed and headed downstairs.

Since her parents were still sleeping and it wouldn't be fair to wake them up, she went downstairs as quietly as she could. She made herself a strong cup of coffee, hoping it would get her out of the funk she was in.

Sandra drove back to her house, determined not to let the way she felt mess up her day. A good run should clear her head. She changed into her running outfit and hit the trail.

Despite having slept only a few hours last night, she pounded the pavement hard, welcoming the smell of freshly cut grass. Someone on her block was mowing their lawn early again.

After about forty minutes, Sandra returned home. The run did her body good, but her mind was still in the doldrums, bogged down by thoughts of Luke.

She took a shower, dressed up for the day and made herself an omelet. Then she made another cup of coffee.

As she lifted her cup to take a sip, her phone started to ring. With trembling hands, she placed the mug down. Sandra looked at the phone, her heart pounding as if she was still running. It was Luke.

Sandra didn't cut off the ringing but gazed at the phone until it stopped. Air she didn't know she was holding rattled out of her lungs as she exhaled.

"Phew, that was close." It had taken a lot from her not to answer the phone.

She took a sip of her coffee and rolled the liquid in her

mouth, proud of herself that she didn't answer the call. Sandra put the mug down, and her phone started to ring again.

A quick glance at the screen told her it was Luke. Sandra took a deep breath and let it out through her mouth. Then she picked up her mug and walked to the living room, her phone still ringing in the kitchen.

37

Luke

Luke slept only about an hour last night. He would have gone jogging, but he knew he had to act fast to begin making amends, to find a way to make it good.

He took a shower, went to his closet to get dressed, and realized he had only one clean pair of jeans and one T-shirt, no underwear. He went commando.

Luke gathered the rest of his dirty clothes, holding his breath as the whiff of his sweat-soaked outfit from last night drifted up to his nose. He walked over to the closet marked laundry and opened it. The washer and dryer were stacked one on top of the other.

"Neat."

On a rack in the closet was a container of detergent pods and an in-wash scent booster. He tossed in a pod and a quarter cap of scent booster, followed by his clothes.

Luke turned the washer on and went to the kitchen. Soon

the rumbling of the washer as it started to do its job faded into the background.

Luke made coffee and checked the time on the machine. He guessed Sandra would be getting ready to go for a run.

He remembered the hurt on her face and wondered if she would be up to going to the restaurant today. He decided to give her more time.

Luke reread his father's journal and bounced around ideas on how to get Sandra back.

He must own the fact that it was him that was the source of the problem and had always been him.

Sandra had always wanted him to do an exhibition, to put his work out there. "You are exceptionally good at what you do," she would say. But it went in one ear and out the other.

He continued to brainstorm, to think of ways to make amends.

After a while, Luke noticed the house was so quiet that he could literally hear his heart beating and the gears twirling in his head. He then realized the washer was done.

He walked over to the closet, transferred his clothes from the washer to the dryer, and turned it on. The rumbling sound of the dryer was comforting.

Back in the living room, Luke looked over at the check. Sandra had always been right. He picked up his phone, took a deep breath, and called her number. It rang through to voicemail. He called her back. Again, it went to voicemail.

Luke didn't want to leave a message. He wanted to speak to her himself. But also, he didn't want to become a stalker or exhibit stalker-like tendencies. It doesn't take much effort from there to slip into the dark side.

It was apparent to Luke she didn't want to speak with him. Was going about this the wrong way? Words are good, but actions are even better.

She'd always wanted him to put his work out there. It would speak for itself, and the rest would take care of itself, she would say.

Luke glanced at the check again, and something clicked in his head. His pulse started to race.

Do an exhibition of his works.

"Yes!" Luke pumped a fist in the air. He would put out his entire portfolio. Show Sandra that he had really changed. First things first, how did he organize an exhibition? Only one name came to mind. Mrs. Paterson.

The gears in Luke's mind started to turn. He wasn't going to call her; he would go and see her. And if he had to get on his knees and crawl across a field of burning charcoals to get her help, so be it.

A plan started to come together fast in his mind.

A loud buzz from somewhere in the house pierced the silence. Luke nearly achieved levitation from the couch. "What the-"

Heart pounding, his eyes darted around, wondering if something had exploded in the kitchen.

It was followed by silence. The constant rumbling in the background had stopped. Luke sighed, realizing the sound must have come from the dryer.

He walked over to the closet and opened it, still expecting to see smoke or something. But everything was fine. He looked at the controls. The cycle was done, and he noticed the knob was turned to alarm. He let out a sigh and turned it off. That sound had given him a real scare.

Luke opened the machine and pulled out his powder blue button-down shirt. It was hot and crisp. It would go well with the white T-shirt and blue jeans he had on already.

Ten minutes later, Luke was in his car driving down Main Street. He pulled into The Glass Flower Shop.

An old lady wearing round spectacles and an apron over her dress watered flowers hanging outside the store. She smiled at Luke as he approached.

"Hello, good morning," said Luke.

"Young man, hello to you too. How can I help you?"

Luke glanced at the flowers. "I'm going to the cemetery to visit my parents, and I wonder what an appropriate bundle would be to lay on their graves."

The woman placed a hand on her chest. "Oh, I'm so sorry for your loss."

Luke smiled. "Thank you…It's been a while."

"True, the immediate hurt gets better with time, but the void is still there." She looked at the flowers on display on the black plastic flower stand. "Hmm, let's see."

He made up his mind to pick the first flowers she pointed to. He liked the ones she was watering. And asked what they were.

"Oh, these are carnations." She pointed at the ones she'd just watered. "They signify love and affection."

"I'll take them!" Luke said. They fit right into the narrative he had in his head.

His father's mad love for his mother had sent him down the part of disaffection for his child while his mother's love for her unborn son made her spare his life. It was all about love.

After he paid and was about to leave, the lady said, "You're Dave's son, right? I've seen you with Sandra."

Luke nodded. There was no need asking which Dave.

"I saw your paintings at the library. Excellent job. I'm rooting for you."

"Thank you."

She waved at him as he drove away.

The cemetery was on the grounds of the church. Apart

from birds chirping and the faint deep sound of trucks on the highway, it was empty and quiet. The graves were laid out like an assorted chocolate box.

Luke laid the flowers, one bouquet on each grave. His father had bought a plot for himself right next to his wife. Both of them lay side by side, finally together.

Luke was not a prayerful person, so he spoke to his parents. He thanked his mother for her love and the gift of art.

He told his father that he now understood why it was hard for him to show affection to him. "I forgive you, Father."

Luke felt like the shackles binding him had been removed after he uttered those words to his father.

Luke checked the time as he walked back to his car. The library would open in five minutes. He hoped Mrs. Paterson would be there and didn't have any other plans that might take her away from the library today.

"So when did you realize that you'd fallen in love with Sandra again?" asked Laura Paterson.

Luke pulled at the collar of his shirt, feeling hot around the neck. Laura had dropped in to see her mother, and when she saw Luke she'd decided to stay a little longer.

Luke had run out of places to look as he tried to avoid eye contact with Laura and her mother. They sat around a table in the same part of the library where just yesterday, a few hours ago, his paintings with those of others had been on display.

Luke repeated the question to buy time. "When did I realize I'd fallen in love again with Sandra?"

"Exactly," said Mrs. Paterson.

Where was he going to start? When he had his fingers up her pussy that first night and she came for him? Or when she sucked him off in her bedroom? What about when they made love in her car, in the woods, swimming pool, etc. Or the last time right under their noses in her parents' house, he was in love. But he couldn't tell them that.

"I've always loved her," said Luke.

"Really? I'm a bit confused," said Mrs. Paterson. "That's not what I saw last night in the parking lot outside."

Luke let out a deep breath. "After the fiasco of yesterday, for lack of a better word. I found new information, did some soul searching, and learned a few things about myself that were not complimentary. Sandra has always been there for me, and I failed to see it."

Laura raised an eyebrow. "Aren't you about to skip town?"

"That's part of the problem. I'd hurt Sandra before, and I was just about to do it again. Now she won't even take my call."

Mrs. Paterson waved to a man who was staring at them. "Nothing to see here, Buddy."

The man turned red and moved away.

Mrs. Paterson turned back to face Luke. "So what do you want to do about it?"

"I want to be here for her, but I don't think she will believe me because of the past." Luke took a deep breath and exhaled. "Sandra has always asked me to do an exhibition, and I always said no. If I did one now, that would help convince her that she has penetrated-"

"Penetrated?" said Mrs. Paterson, making a face.

"Pierced the veil…no, no." Luke raised his hand. "Made me see sense."

Laura and her mom exchanged glances.

Laura said, "So this change of heart, was it after you saw the check from the art sale, or before?"

Luke swallowed. "It would seem like I got the money and

now know I could make more if I exhibited. I know that's a potential problem I would face."

Laura moved her head from side to side. "Ummm...yeah! That's exactly what it seems like. It's like porn! You know it when you see it."

"I know it's hard to believe because of what happened in the past, but please give me a chance. I don't want to lose her again. I know Peter's in play, but I don't care. I want to give getting her back my best shot. If he's who she wants, then I don't have any choice but to back away. Her happiness is all I care for."

The two women were quiet. The silence was so thick you could hang your hat on it.

Luke forced a laugh. "I understand if you can't help me. Thanks for your time. I'll go over to the restaurant or her house and talk to her." Luke made to get up.

"Sit your butt down," said Mrs. Paterson. "Men!" she muttered under her breath, shaking her head. "Look here, Luke. Sandra doesn't want to see you right now."

"You're not exactly her favorite person at the moment," said Laura. She looked at her mother, and they exchanged glances.

Mrs. Paterson nodded. "Okay, we'll help you with the exhibition. Matters of the heart are out of our realm of influence. But we can put in a word or two. We're counting on you not to let us down and break her heart again if we succeed in swaying her."

"Thank you so much." Luke didn't know whether to hug them or kiss them. "This means so much to me!"

"We have another exhibition planned in two days," said Mrs. Paterson. She cocked her head. "Hmm...that is tomorrow." She exhaled. "It's not too much time. Just bring all your work over this morning."

Luke was relieved. So far, so good. He decided to drive to his house, bring the paintings, and do whatever he could to set things in motion.

As he drove to the Airbnb, he drove past a one-story office building he'd always passed. A particular notice board he must have seen a thousand times caught his eyes and got him thinking.

Luke went home, loaded all his paintings in the car, and headed back for the library.

As he neared the one-story building again, he didn't think twice. He drove into the parking lot.

Minutes later, Luke walked into the building. He stopped at the door with a plaque that read, *Mossberg and Mulberry, Attorneys at Law.*

38

Sandra

SANDRA WAS HOME, TRYING TO RELAX IN SHORTS AND AN oversized T-shirt. She curled up on the sofa in her living room, watching a rerun of *Friends* on the TV as background noise.

Why does love hurt so much?

She twirled a spoon around the surface of a vanilla chocolate chip ice cream on which she'd sprinkled some honey nut granola.

Sandra had been saving it for a day like this which she believed would never come, but here we are.

She scooped a teaspoon of the creamy goodness into her mouth, letting it sit for a few seconds on her tongue to melt a little before she started to chew. She froze when her doorbell rang.

Who could it be? Amazon? She hadn't ordered anything lately.

Oh God. She hoped it wasn't Luke. He'd called a few times earlier in the morning and then gave it a break.

Sandra tiptoed to the window and discreetly looked out. "What?" Her mood lightened. She went over to the door, unlocked it, and threw it open.

"Nobody told me I was hosting a mother-daughter reunion!"

Sally and Laura stormed into her living room. Within a few minutes of arriving, they'd made themselves at home. They all sat in her living room. Sally nursed a mug of coffee while Laura confiscated Sandra's ice cream for herself.

"This is contraband, you know," said Laura as another scoop disappeared in her mouth.

"So let's get down to the reason why we're here," said Sally.

Sandra shrugged. "I'm not on my death bed, you know. Just a little matter of the heart that will heal with time."

Sally put down her coffee. "We're having a Luke Martin, local artist exhibit tomorrow. And-"

Sandra's eyes widened. "What?"

"Because of the unique role you played in making it possible, we're here personally to invite you to attend."

"He finally agreed to exhibit his work?" asked Sandra, her voice a high squeak. She shook her head. "I can't believe it."

Sandra stood with her hands resting on her hips akimbo. "This is just unbelievable."

Then she started to nod. "Of course. It's all about money-the check. Well, the answer is no! You know what he told me last night? That was the last straw. That I never mind my own business. Now he sees the check, and all of a sudden, he has a change of heart."

"Sandra, I know what you've been through," said Laura.

"And I'm sorry for the part I played that first day he showed up, but he says he's changed. He said you mean the world to him…"

Sally got up and walked over to Sandra. "Listen, men are douchebags."

Sandra's eyes found the floor. What was she going to do? She'd thought this was over, that he'd pack his things and head back to California.

Sally continued, "But this douchebag came to us on his knees. He confessed that you've always insisted on him exhibiting his work, and he always brushed you off. He said this was the only way he knew to prove to you that he'd changed."

"We brought up the money issue too," said Laura, standing and walking over to Sandra.

Sandra's eyes shot up. "You did?"

Laura touched Sandra's shoulder. "Of course money is a great motivator. He said it wasn't, but at the end of the day, we're not in his heart and can only hope for the better."

"Look at it this way," said Sally. "This first in a lifetime exhibition of Luke Martin's work wouldn't have come to pass if it weren't for you. It will bring publicity to Beaver Run, the library, and to Beaver Tail too. I know he's hurt you, but you're coming for us."

Sandra's voice cracked. "It hurts." All the tears she'd been fighting hard not to shed finally started coming like a torrential rainfall.

Laura hugged her. "It's okay. I'll be there too…by your side." She rubbed her back. "We can leave the library whenever you want. We still have to work at the restaurant, right?"

Sandra laughed. "Okay," she said, her voice choked with tears.

39

Luke

LUKE WAS NERVOUS. DESPITE THE MOTIVATION AND HIS commitment to exhibit his work, the fears and inadequacies he felt did not just vanish overnight.

He was glad he'd done laundry the day before, giving him more options of what to wear. Today he wore slacks, a white shirt, and a pair of loafers. He'd brought in a piece of work in a box.

"It's my masterpiece," said Luke when Mrs. Paterson asked what was in it. He asked for a pedestal, which was provided, and he placed the box on it.

Luke hoped Sandra would come. Today would be his best chance to prove to her that he'd changed.

Mrs. Paterson went all out for the planning of the exhibition. Even the local newspaper was there, and they interviewed him. She assured him that people from other counties would be coming too.

Luke checked the time on his phone. It was twenty

minutes to the official starting time. He'd been looking out for Sandra and wondered if and when she would come.

He didn't dare ask Laura again if Sandra was coming. He figured he would be devastated if he knew for sure she wasn't. It was better to be hopeful. Hope was the stepping-stone to achieving the desires of your heart.

Right now, standing in the library propped up by caffeine and hope, waiting for the exhibition to start, his mind drifted to the past twenty-four hours.

Once Luke left the attorney's office, he'd driven straight to the library and brought the paintings in. Then he went to the librarian's office.

He found Mrs. Paterson in her office, working the phones, sending emails and text messages to make sure that it would be well attended.

When Luke informed her he was offering forty percent of each sale to the library as commission, including the one they sold to Mr. Murphy, the phone slipped out of her hand.

"My God, we were already doing it for nothing."

"Well," said Luke, "if it wasn't for the library and you, it would be forty percent of nothing."

For the first time since he came back to Beaver Run, he found Mrs. Paterson struggling with what to say.

Finally, she blurted out, "Thank you."

"No, thank you," said Luke.

Mrs. Paterson screamed for another staff member to start working on their social media. "We need to fill this library with bodies."

Luke worked with Mrs. Paterson and some other library staff to set up the easels in the same area as the previous exhibition. He'd come up with names for all the paintings, including the accurate sizes of each canvas.

Sarah, Trevor's wife, was there. She helped with the setup, reassuring him that his paintings were amazing.

"I used to work for a billionaire, and the paintings he had on his walls were good. But these are mind-blowing." She paused. "How long did it take you to produce them?"

At the barbecue, he'd overheard some guests say she was the coolest millionaire they knew. Luke wanted to ask her what type of work she did before, working for someone else that made her millions.

Instead, Luke said, "That's my life's work. Most I produced in the past four years during my wanderings." He looked at her. "The theme of the paintings is obvious, right?"

Sarah smiled. "American landscapes."

Luke nodded.

Later that afternoon, Mrs. Paterson said to him, "Get out of here and get some rest. You'll be doing a lot of standing and talking tomorrow."

Luke left, stopped at the Glass Gift Shop, and bought some supplies. Back home, he went to work on the masterpiece. He stumbled into bed in the early hours of the morning.

A loud 'Hello' pulled him out of his reverie.

Luke looked up just as Sandra walked through the door and hugged Mrs. Paterson. She wore an above-the-knee sundress that hugged her in all the right places. Her blond hair was let down to her shoulders. God, she was beautiful.

Beside her was Laura, similarly dressed as Sandra with a different print and color to her outfit. She waved at Luke, and as she lowered her hand, gave him a discreet thumbs-up.

Luke's heart leaped with joy. Seeing Sandra was enough for him, even if the rest of the day ended up in the toilet. All the nervousness he felt vanished.

He walked over to Sandra, smiling. He wanted to hug her,

but her body language didn't lend to that. "Thank you for coming. It means so much to me."

Sandra gave him a polite nod, her lips a thin line. She continued moving.

"Hello, Luke," said Laura.

Luke grinned. "Hi." He moved on too, mingling with people. He'd thought Mrs. Paterson would introduce him as the artist. Maybe she forgot. He shrugged it off. After all, he hadn't been here the last time, and people still loved his paintings. In his peripheral view, he noticed a man in uniform coming toward him. He turned.

"Hey, Luke!"

It was the deputy sheriff in full uniform. "Trevor!" Heat rushed to Luke's cheeks. He prayed the floor would open up and swallow him. Only yesterday, he'd tried to pin his missing paintings on his sister. "Hey, thanks so much for coming. I'm so sorry about the other evening."

"Don't worry about that. It was just a misunderstanding." He looked around. "The paintings are amazing-and look at the crowd."

"That's all thanks to Mrs. Paterson, Laura, and Sandra. They know people that know people."

"Well, good luck." Trevor winked at him. "If you need a police escort at the end of the day to safeguard your checks, don't hesitate to ask."

For the next five to ten minutes, Luke walked around, trying to get close to Sandra.

Each time, someone would intercept him with a question, or she would be engaged in conversation with someone. One time she saw him coming and relocated to another part of the exhibition.

People came and went. At one point, a coach, like a Greyhound bus, stopped in front of the library. People poured out of it.

Soon after, Mrs. Paterson introduced Mr. Murphy as the buyer of the landscape nude. Luke thanked him profusely.

"I love the Baroque influence in your paintings," said Mr. Murphy. "Perhaps you are the Caravaggio of the twenty-first century. Keep it up." He moved on.

All around Luke, his works were being considered for purchase, and a few had sold. Popular lore has it that Vincent Van Gogh had sold only one of his paintings during his lifetime.

In his own life so far, he'd sold a lot more of his paintings than Van Gogh. Luke considered himself luckier and in no way close in talent to the art legend.

Fixing prices initially was a problem, but Luke and Mrs. Paterson found a solution that they hoped worked for the buyers too.

When Van Gogh's *Portrait of Dr. Gachet* sold for the world-record price of $82 million in 1990, The Baltimore Sun called his story 'one of the cruelest in the history of art.' Van Gogh died poor in 1890.

The sad truth was that a good number of artists sold very few of their work at a price they could live on.

Just then, Luke caught sight of the attorney. He checked the time on his phone-it had been precisely thirty minutes since the exhibition started. He was right on time.

The lawyer, forehead furrowed, looked around. Then his face relaxed, and he walked toward Sandra.

Luke's pulse raced.

The lawyer handed Sandra an envelope.

She hesitated.

Her eyes drifted down to the envelope, then back to the attorney's face. He said something, then pushed it toward her again. Sandra took it. The attorney smiled, nodded, and left.

Luke's eyes were on Sandra. She took a few steps to the side, opened the envelope, and started to read. Moments later, her head shot up, mouth open.

Her eyes dashed around and settled on Luke. She shook her head vigorously, her lips mouthing the word *no* several times.

Knock! Knock! Knock!

Luke pulled his eyes away. His attention was drawn to the loud sound, like someone knocking on a door. It was Sally.

"Your attention please!" said Sally and struck a table one more time with a paperweight. "Thank you, thank you, thank you!" She smoothed her beige skirt suit, which was a perfect fit. "Thank you all for coming at such short notice, and welcome to Beaver Run Library!"

People clapped and cheered.

Mrs. Paterson raised both hands palm out, and the cheer quietened. "Sorry, I'm doing this backward. The introductions should have been made at the beginning of the exhibition."

"Better late than never!" someone yelled.

People laughed.

"Due to popular demand, we brought back THE gem of Beaver Run. A young artist who grew up here and is known for his breathtaking oil on canvas landscapes…and"—she lowered her voice—"his nudes."

Someone made a catcall.

Mrs. Paterson pointed to Luke. "Ladies and gentlemen, I present to you Luke Martin, the painter."

Luke's heart vibrated like a jackhammer in his chest. He took a few steps and was beside the pedestal with the box containing his masterpiece.

Luke scanned the room, and his eyes met Sandra's. Hers were as wide as saucers, and she mouthed the word *no*, shaking her head fervently.

Luke pulled his eyes away from her. He was going to do it. He looked at the people, smiled, then cleared his throat.

40

Sandra

SANDRA STOOD IN THE LIBRARY WATCHING THE MAN SHE'D loved forever about to make the greatest mistake of his life.

She'd only come because of Laura and Sally. As far as she was concerned, Luke was a lost cause. He knew what he wanted and only wanted her for sport. He was mixing up lust for love.

Sandra knew he might say yesterday was all a mistake, the devil's work. Could she find it in herself to forgive and forget?

He'd already sent Sally and Laura to her. They'd won her over, but right now, she'd girded her loins. Whatever he pitched to her right now, she must hit it back to him, or even out of the park...library—a home run.

Things had been going fine at the exhibition until Mr. Mulberry, the junior attorney at Mossberg and Mulberry, Attorneys at Law, had walked up to her.

Sandra knew him. When she'd bought into the bar and

restaurant, she had used their services to write up the business papers.

Her thoughts drifted back to that moment mere minutes ago. At first, she thought the paper Mr. Mulberry thrust in her hand was a subpoena. Maybe somebody had gotten drunk at the bar, gotten in an accident, and was now suing her.

But when she opened it, she couldn't believe her eyes as she read the text on the cream-colored rich, thick paper, with the attorney's office letterhead embossed on it.

The letter read, '*I, Luke Martin, in good health and of clear mind, bestow to Sandra Leigh of Beaver Run, New Jersey, all the paintings or proceeds from the sale of the paintings listed below.*'

He went ahead and listed all the paintings that were on display with their dimensions. Sandra gasped. Why would he do such a thing?

She couldn't accept it. Was Luke now trying to buy her?

Sandra raised her head, and their eyes met. He was looking at her. She mouthed the word *no*.

Luke smiled and looked away, ignoring her.

Sandra knew there was more to come. Then Sally started banging on the table.

Luke's voice brought her back to the present.

"Thank you for coming. I'm humbled by the turnout and the faith the people of Beaver Run and all invited guests have in me. I thank especially Mrs. Paterson, Laura Paterson, and Sandra Leigh, to mention but a few." He pointed at each one as he spoke their name. "Especially Sandra Leigh."

"Beaver Tail, yeah!" someone yelled.

Sandra felt lightheaded, like she was about to faint. She sucked in air. Too many emotions. That feeling subsided and was quickly replaced by a tingling that swept across her neck to her face.

"Yes, that's the best bar in town," said Luke. "Not to take up too much of your time, I'll cut to the chase. I came into town two weeks ago for the first time in a long time. It was like the return of the prodigal son. My car broke down in front of Beaver Tail."

"Oh, that sucks," said a big-boned dirty woman with dirty-blond hair, with a colossal backpack strapped to her back. She wore tiny shorts and an oversized T-shirt.

Some folks giggled.

"Providence," said Sally.

"I agree," said Luke. He turned to the backpack lady. "Yes, it did suck."

Then to Sally, he nodded. "Providence too! The unseen hand that guides our every move. I had no idea Sandra was there, but there she was, and we reunited after four years."

Some people clapped.

Asshole, thought Sandra. They'd united only after she offered him free pussy for two weeks. Even a celibate monk would find that challenging to walk away from.

Luke continued. "I've been in love with Sandra since we were in high school."

"In lust," said Sandra under her breath, shaking her head. She refocused on the piece of paper in her hand and shook her head in despair. Luke was making a mistake.

Luke continued. "She's always had my best interest at heart, always believed in me. I was opposed to exhibiting my work. Her pleas to me to do so fell on deaf ears." Luke paused.

Sandra looked up.

"Then she took matters into her own hands," said Luke, "and showed the world my work, what I could do. A few days ago, I said some hurtful things to her." Luke turned to Sandra. "I'm so sorry. I beg for your forgiveness."

All eyes were on Sandra. She didn't know what to do. She wasn't going to fall for his shenanigans again.

But how was she going to extract herself from the people here, who were obviously in Luke's camp? Luke's next action gave her some breathing room.

Luke walked over to the pedestal with a covered box. "I started working on this two days ago…from memory." He unwrapped the box as he spoke. "It's not finished yet, but almost there." Luke removed the box.

Sandra's hands flew to her mouth.

People gasped.

It was a sculpture of Sandra's bust.

Sandra knew Luke had gifted hands-a shudder ran through her as she remembered his hands stroking her like guitar strings, but this…

Warmth spread out from her girly parts outward. Luke's hands would never go there again. She would never let it happen.

From the corners of her eyes, she saw people taking quick side glances at her.

The woman with the backpack that spoke up earlier pointed at the clay bust. "It's her! It's her!" Her voice was a loud whisper.

Sandra hated the woman, a busybody who wouldn't mind her own business. She focused on the statue as Luke continued to speak.

Sandra was amazed by Luke's craftsmanship. His attention to detail. Nobody had ever sculpted her before or sketched her, apart from him. He'd caught her likeness, to the little nuances of her nose and eyes.

In the sculpture, her left hand rested on her neck, and the middle finger had a yellowish band…what? Sandra's heart missed a beat. Oh God please, no.

A whoosh, whoosh, whoosh sound filled her ears as blood rushed through her head.

Let that not be what she thought it was. But she knew it was. Nope, she was not going to accept it. Sandra's whole body rejected it.

The question would come soon. Sandra girded herself. She didn't want to say no and embarrass him in front of all these people. Nor say yes, to what she didn't believe in—something she would regret.

Sandra felt a tightness around her chest, like a piece of wet cloth being wrung. She had to get out of here, but the golden band seemed to have hypnotized her. She couldn't pull her eyes away from it.

"Wait!" said the woman with the backpack and stepped in front of Sandra to get closer to the bust.

Luke stopped in mid-sentence.

"Is that a real ring?" asked the woman.

She'd completely blocked Sandra's view from the sculpture.

Sandra could breathe again. She filled her lungs, turned, and hustled for the exit. Behind her, she could hear Luke addressing the woman.

"Yes," said Luke. "It belonged to a woman who refused lifesaving cancer treatment so that her unborn child could live. She sacrificed herself-unconditional love. I was that child, and the woman, my mother."

A murmur broke out among the attendees.

Luke continued. "Today, there's a woman right here that has loved me without question. She's always been there for me. She's walked on thin ice for me more times than I can count. I want to tell her that I love her and appreciate her love and would be the happiest person if she would have me." Luke removed the ring from the sculpture's finger. "I want to give that same ring to a woman I love unconditionally…"

"Awhh," went the crowd.

Luke said, "Could you…move to the side. I…I think she's behind you."

People laughed.

Sandra was a few feet from the exit. She walked faster.

41

Luke

LUKE HAD BEEN WORRIED ABOUT CONVINCING SANDRA THAT it wasn't the check for the painting that had motivated him to have a change of heart. The idea to 'will' all his paintings to her would, he believed, be a strong indication that he didn't care about them-it was her he cared about.

She'd been thin-lipped after the lawyer left.

It would be reasonable to say she looked upset. Luke reckoned she would get over it, and once he proposed, things would be smooth sailing.

Luke watched Sandra when he unveiled the sculpture. He noted the surprise on her face change to subtle joy. Then the backpack lady brought up the engagement ring, giving him a reason to talk about it, then propose.

But as he spoke to her, he noticed the shift in Sandra's face to what looked like terror. Then the lady had blocked his view of her. The next time he saw her, she was swiftly walking toward the exit, then she went through the door.

Luke wanted to run after her right away, but the blond lady kept him pinned down with more questions.

"So what was your mother like?" asked the woman.

"She was a lovely soul and passed just after I was born," said Luke. He tried to remain calm. "She could have saved herself and not gone through with the pregnancy." Luke made to leave.

"Was she an artist too?" asked the same woman.

"Yes." Luke raised his hand. "I'll be right back." He headed for the door exit and rushed outside. *Please let her still be there*, he said to himself.

The bright morning sunlight hit him. He placed his hand on his forehead and scanned the parking lot. He saw Sandra standing beside her truck, talking to Laura.

Luke approached them. "Sandra, are you okay?"

"Hi, Luke," said Laura. She turned to Sandra. "I won't be far away." Her voice was low. She squeezed Sandra's hand and walked toward the library.

Sandra held up the envelope and letter clutched in her fist. "Luke, what is this? What is this?"

Her eyes brimmed with unshed tears.

Luke was at first confused. He recognized the paper and the letterhead. He was about to say just that, then stopped himself. It wasn't what she wanted to know. It was the why.

"You can't buy love," said Sandra, her voice filled with tears. "I'm not even selling love. You…you are not even in love with me. You just feel sorry for me…you…you feel you owe me. You don't owe me anything. I went in with my eyes open. You've had your fill, so did I, and we called it quits. Why…why this? Don't insult me with this." She threw the document back at him.

"No…Sandra, no. I'm so sorry. I didn't mean to upset

you. I love you, Sandra, but something inside me kept on making me push you away."

She stood there watching him, her chest rising and falling, tears rolling down her cheeks.

Luke felt encouraged and continued. "Sandra, you've always been there for me. Before I saw the check, I read my father's journal. It was in the bag we brought back from the storage unit. I found out the reason why he hated me so much. He believed my mother chose me over him. He loved her so much, and I was a constant reminder of what he'd lost."

Luke sighed. "He just couldn't bring himself to show me love, neither could he get rid of me."

Luke took a step closer to her. "All my life, I felt like I was a failure…that I did something wrong, that made him stop caring. Instead of waiting for people to stop loving me just as my father did, I leave before they get a chance to push me away."

Sandra folded her hands over her chest, hugging herself as if she were cold.

"You're the world to me. I can't hide my track record. I messed up! It's there for all to see. I abandoned you before and was about to do it again. The only way I felt I could convince you was by giving you the very things I hold dear and proposing to you."

Luke's eyesight turned cloudy, but he dared not blink.

Tears poured down Sandra's face.

Luke shook his head. "I'm so sorry for all the hurt I've caused you." His voice was quiet. "I hope you can forgive me and take me back."

Sandra wiped her eyes with the back of her hand.

"You mean the world to me."

She stood there looking at him, crying silently.

Luke knew he had lost her.

Sandra's lips quivered. "Oh Luke. Are...are you sure?"

Luke cocked his head. "Am I sure?"

"I don't want you to freak out and leave me again. My heart can't take any more strain."

"Sandra, I can't afford to lose you again. I can't imagine a life without you. I'm sure, Sandra. You complete me and mean the world to me."

She looked into his eyes, then smiled. "Okay."

Luke spread out his hand, and she rushed in. They kissed and kissed and kissed. "I love you so much, Sandra."

"Me too."

Luke drew back and dipped his hand into his pocket. Moments later, the engagement ring appeared. He dropped to one knee.

"No, no, no," said Sandra. She grabbed Luke's hands. "Get up, get up!" she hissed. "People are watching." She pulled him up.

Luke got to his feet and looked around. She was right. People stood by the library door watching and looked away when he looked at them. "I don't want to lose you for any reason...to Peter or anyone else."

Sandra tossed her head back and laughed. "I'm sorry I deceived you. There's nothing between Peter and me. I only wanted to get back at you."

Sandra kissed him. "We just got back together." She kissed him again. "One step at a time."

EPILOGUE

Five Months later

Sandra drove past Sam Stone's Airbnb on her way back to her place. Each time she drove by, she remembered that first night she'd gone to drop off Luke when he arrived at Beaver Run five months ago.

She glanced at the house. The lights were on. It seemed like it had an occupant, probably overflow from people vacationing in Mountain Peak.

Just looking at the place had her hot and bothered. She'd heard about the 1890s experiment by the Russian physiologist Ivan Pavlov. He'd researched salivation in dogs in response to being fed and found out that just ringing a bell alone at that time when he fed the dogs resulted in them salivating.

For Sandra, just passing the house where Luke's busy fingers had given her a mind-blowing orgasm got her panties all wet. She was going to ride that cock once she got home.

Sandra giggled. She'd become a nymphomaniac. She just couldn't get enough of this man. They were like teenagers all over again. They were so lucky, she reminded herself. Falling in love with your best friend was the stuff of romance novels.

Luke had offered to stay on at Stone's place without moving in with Sandra. Beaver Run was a small town, and they would be seen as living in sin. He just didn't want people to talk and argued that the house had excellent lighting.

Sandra wouldn't have any of that. "Let them talk. I don't want you out of my sight again. Unless that speech you gave at the library about me completing you was all talk."

Luke complied immediately. "I can paint from anywhere," he had said. "The room with the most natural light would be the best."

That was her spare bedroom, so they turned it into a studio, and Luke moved in.

Sandra's phone buzzed, distracting her from her reverie. It was a text from Luke. He had a surprise for her and wanted her to hurry home. A shiver ran down Sandra's spine. The last time he'd sent her such a text, he had laid out candles, stripped her naked, and massaged her from head to toe with massage oil that left her skin glowing and tingling all over.

Sandra tossed her phone on the passenger seat and relived the previous experience.

His instruction to her was not to touch him or use her hands on herself. He had practiced edging on her. Bring her to the brink of climax with his fingers and lips, then backing away.

After an hour, she was begging him to make her come. Then she failed and obliged herself with her fingers.

"Next time, I'll tie you up," Luke had said.

Maybe that was the surprise, thought Sandra. Her phone dinged again. She ignored it.

Since the last time she'd updated her phone, each message dinged twice. What the hell?

The house was toasty warm when Sandra got home. The seven-foot Christmas tree close to the fireplace, twinkled, and Christmas music played softly in the background from surround Bluetooth speakers.

Sandra peeled off her warm layers, her scarf followed by her jacket. She unhooked her bra and tossed it aside. She reached under her sweater, squeezed, and massaged her breasts.

She couldn't wait for Luke's hands to get on them. She stopped, sat down and on the couch, and took off her boots. She removed her leggings, peeled off her soaked panties, and tossed them to the side.

Sandra opened the door to the studio, and her heart stopped.

"About time you got back, young lady!" said her father.

Her mom sighed. "You've had us waiting for so long." She looked at Sandra from head to toe. "Don't tell me you went out like that?"

"All right, Luke," said Trevor, getting up from a chair. "What's the big surprise? I have to get back to the office."

"Oh God," said Sandra in a whisper. She raised her hand to her mouth. Her sweater rode up. She felt a chill on her butt and lowered her hands.

"Sandra! Naughty, naughty!"

It was her sister Alexis's voice.

Sandra whirled around. Alexis and Sarah were at the doorway behind her.

"Hi Sandra," said Sarah and waved.

Her whole family was here.

Luke spoke through the corner of his lips. "Sweetie, you didn't get my text."

Sandra tried to speak but couldn't find the words.

"Get on with it!" barked her father.

"Yes, sir," said Luke. "Ummm, thank you all for coming at such short notice. It's something I've been working on for a while. It's finally finished." He walked Sandra over to an object covered with a piece of cloth.

"What are you doing?" asked Sandra.

Luke pulled the cloth off.

Sandra gasped.

"Wow! It's Sandra," said her dad. "I always knew it. You're better than that guy that married my sister."

"I've been working on it for some time," said Luke. "I finally finished it."

Alexis pointed. "What's that on the middle finger?"

Luke feigned surprise. "What?" He removed the ring and dropped to one knee. "Sandra Leigh. I'm so much in love with you. I can't bear to see another Christmas without making this official. Will you marry me?"

Sandra's heart was pounding in her chest like a washing machine that just started on a spinning cycle. "Yes, yes, I'll marry you."

"Congratulations!" they all said at the same time.

Her whole family applauded.

"About time," said Sandra's mom.

"You guys should spend Christmas in Paris," said Alexis. "The city of love."

"Okay," said Sandra, wanting them to get going.

Two hours later, her whole family had left, and Sandra had Luke all cuffed up and having her way with him. She'd been working him up for about an hour.

Luke's hands were secured with fluffy handcuffs.

"Why didn't you warn me?" said Sandra.

"I did. It wasn't my fault you didn't check your phone a second time."

Sandra looked at his naked body on the bed and giggled.

"What…what's funny?" asked Luke.

"Your cock kind of reminds me of the Eiffel Tower."

Luke's cock twitched. "Well, we'll be going there for Christmas…"

For the past fifty minutes, she'd been riding him, and disembarking once she felt he was about to reach an orgasm.

"Sweetheart," said Luke. His voice was tight, full of want. "Why don't you mount the Eiffel Tower again, and this time ride faster to the top?" Luke groaned. "Please, Sandra, let me come. I can't take it anymore."

"Not yet. You embarrassed me in front of my family, and you deserve every punishment you get." She climbed on top of him and lowered herself, his cock sliding into her wet pussy. She leaned forward and brushed her nipples against his lips.

Luke moaned. "Oh, that feels good." With both hands still secured to the headboard with cuffs, he raised his torso and captured one nipple with his mouth. He nibbled hard.

Sandra moaned. "Yes, suck it."

Luke obliged her.

Sandra started slowly, raising her hips and lowering them with his cock impaled inside her. Slowly, she built up the pace, faster and faster.

"Yes, don't stop," said Luke with a groan. "Baby…make me come." He pushed up his pelvis to meet hers. The flap, flap, flap of skin slapping skin filled the room.

Sandra wanted to stop, but she too had passed the point of no return. She gasped as her orgasm caught her by surprise and tore her apart. She came and came and came.

Luke moaned. "Oh yes baby…I'm…." His body shook as

an explosive climax tore through him. "I love you, Sandra Leigh, forever."

The End.

Laura's story – Single mother, Second Chance, 2 Exes coming soon!! To be notified when its ready, click follow on BookBub below.

Follow me on BookBub to learn more

ALSO BY BRIE WILDS

The Stark Brother Series

Should I Say Yes

Never Been Loved

Love is Patient

The Stark Brothers Box Set

Cupid Cabana Series

Cupid Came Through

Maid for Him

Blame Cupid

Mountain Peak Series

The Neighbor Who Stole Christmas

Sleighing the Billionaire

Three Wise Men for Christmas

Beaver Run Series

Sarah's Secret

Kissed and Forgotten

My Big Fat Fake Matrimonial Ad

Beaver Run Reunion Series

Unbreak Her Heart

JOIN MY NEWSLETTER

Want to receive the latest information on my upcoming novels and receive a FREE book? Sign up for my free author newsletter by clicking on Brie Wilds Newsletter or visit www.briewilds.com

CPSIA information can be obtained
at www.ICGtesting.com
Printed in the USA
BVHW031546310521
608476BV00007B/235

ABOUT THE AUTHOR

Brie Wilds is the author of My Big Fat Fake Matrimonial Ad, Book 3 of her Beaver Run Series. *Beaver Run* is a series of stand-alone, small-town, interconnected romance stories. Each book promises a complete, sweet, steamy, and happily ever after story.

Brie writes steamy, romance stories about men and women and their amazing and unique journey to finding happily ever after. Visit her website at www.briewilds.com for a free gift.